I0669191

Reprint Publishing

FOR PEOPLE WHO GO FOR ORIGINALS.

www.reprintpublishing.com

"ALL ABOARD FOR SLEEP," SAID JIMIEBOY.

Half-Hours With Jimmieboy.

BY

JOHN KENDRICK BANGS,

AUTHOR OF

"Tiddledywink Tales," "In Camp with a Tin Soldier,"
"Tiddledywink Poetry Book," etc.

ILLUSTRATED BY

FRANK VERBECK, CHARLES HOWARD JOHNSON,
J. T. RICHARDS, P. NEWELL,
AND OTHERS.

NEW YORK:
R. H. RUSSELL & SON,
MDCCCXCIII.

TO MY SON,

FRANCIS HYDE BANGS.

Thanks are due to Messrs. Harper & Bros. for the
privilege of re-printing several of the
stories in this book.

CONTENTS.

I.

CHRISTMAS EVE AT JIMMIEBOY'S.

IT had been a long and trying day to Jimmie-boy, as December 24th usually is to children of his age, who have great expectations, and are more or less impatient to have them fulfilled. He had been positively cross at supper-time because his father had said that Santa Claus had written to say that a much-desired veloci-pede could not be got down through the chimney, and that he thought Jimmieboy would have to wait until the chimneys had been enlarged, or his papa had built a new house with more commodious flues.

"I think it's just too bad," said Jimmieboy, as he climbed into bed an hour later. "Just be-cause those chimneys are small, I can't have a philocipede, and I've been gooder than ever for two weeks, just to get it."

Then, as his nurse extinguished the lamp and went into the adjoining room to sew, Jimmieboy threw himself back upon his pillow and shed a tear. The tear crept slowly down over his cheek, and was about to disappear between his lips and go back again to where it had started from, when a voice was heard over by the fire-place.

"Can you get it down?" it said.

Jimmieboy sat up and peered over toward the spot whence the voice came, but could see nothing.

"No. The hind wheels won't go through the chimney-pot, and even if they would, it wouldn't do any good. The front wheel is twice as big as the hind ones," said another voice, this one apparently belonging to some one on the roof. "Can't you get it in through the front door?"

"What do you take me for—an expressman?" cried the voice at the fire-place. "I can't leave things that way. It wouldn't be the proper thing. Can't you get a smaller size through?"

"Yes; but will it fit the boy?" said the voice on the roof.

"Lower your lantern down here and we'll see. He's asleep over here in a brass bedstead," replied the other.

And then Jimmieboy saw a great red lantern appear in the fire-place, and by its light he noticed a short, ruddy-faced, merry-eyed old gentleman, with a snowy beard and a smile, tip-toeing across the room toward him. To his de-light he recognized him at once as Santa Claus; but he didn't know whether Santa Claus would like to have him see him or not, so he closed his eyes as tightly as he could, and pretended to be asleep.

"Humph!" ejaculated Santa Claus, as he leaned over Jimmieboy's bed, and tried to get his measure by a glance. "He's almost a man— must be five years old by this time. Pretty big for a small velocipede; still, I don't know." Here he scratched his beard and sang:

"If he's too large for it, I think,
'Twill be too small for him,
Unless he can be got to shrink
Two inches on each limb."

Then he walked back to the fire-place and called out, "I've measured."

"Well, what's the result?" queried the voice on the roof.

"'Nothing,' as the boy said when he was asked what two plus one minus three amounted to. I can't decide. It will or it won't, and that's all there is about it."

"Can't we try it on him?" asked the voice up the chimney.

"No," returned Santa Claus. "That wouldn't prove anything; but we might try him on it. Shall I send him up?"

"Yes," came the voice from above, much to Jimmieboy's delight, for he was quite curious to see what was going on up on the roof, and who it was that owned the other voice.

In a moment Jimmieboy found himself in Santa Claus's arms, cuddled up to the warm fur coat the dear old gentleman wore, in which position he was carried up through the chimney flue to the roof. Then Jimmieboy peeped out between his half-opened eyelids, and saw, much to his surprise, that instead of there being only one Santa Claus, there were two of them.

"Oh dear!" he said in astonishment; "I didn't know there were two of you."

Both the Santas jumped as if some one had let off a cannon cracker under their very noses.

"Well, I declare!" said the one that had carried Jimmieboy up through the chimney. "We're discovered. Here I've been in this business whole centuries, and I've never been discovered before."

"That's so," assented the other. "We know now how America must have felt when Columbus came sailing in. What'll we do about it?"

"We'll have to take him into partnership, I

guess," rejoined the first. "It'll never do in this world not to. Would you like to be one of our concern, Jimmieboy?"

"Oh, indeed I would," said Jimmieboy.

"Well, I say we let him help us this time anyhow," said the roof Santa Claus. "You're so fat, I'm afraid you can't get down some of these small chimneys, and Jimmieboy is just about the right size."

"Good scheme," said the other; "but he isn't dressed for it, you know."

"He can get a nice black soot down in the factory chimney," said the roof Santa Claus, with a wink.

"That's so; and as the factory fires are always going, it will be a nice warm soot. What do you say, Jimmieboy?" said the other.

"It's lovely," replied the boy. "But how did there come to be two of you?"

"There had to be," said the first Santa Claus Jimmieboy had seen. "The world is growing so fast that my work has nearly doubled in the last twenty years, so I had to get an assistant, and he did so well, I took him into partnership. He's my brother."

"And is his name Santa Claus, too?" asked Jimmieboy.

"Oh no, indeed. His name is Marmaduke. We call him Marmy for short, and I can tell you what it is, Jimmieboy,

> "He is as fine a fellow
> As ever you did spy;
> He's quite as sweet and mellow,
> Though not so fat as I."

"And that's a recommendation that any man has a right to be proud of," said Marmy Claus, patting himself on the back to show how proud he felt. "But, Santa, we must be off. It would not do for the new firm of Santa, Marmy, and Jimmie Claus to begin business by being late. We've got to leave toys in eighteen flat-houses, forty-two hotels, and an orphan asylum yet."

"That's a fact," said Santa, jumping into the sleigh and grasping the reins. "Just help Jimmieboy in here, Marmy, and we'll be off. We can leave his things here on our way back."

Then, before he knew how it happened, Jimmieboy found himself wrapped up warmly in a great fur coat, with a seal-skin cap on his head, and the dearest, warmest ear-tabs over his ears, sitting in the middle of the sleigh between the two huge. jolly-faced, members of the Claus family. The long lash of the whip snapped in the frosty air, at the sound of which the reindeer sprang forward and dragged the toy-laden cutter off on its aerial flight.

At the start Santa drove, and Marmy prepared the toys for the first little boy they were to visit, handing Jimmieboy a lot of sugar-plums, to keep him from getting hungry, before he began.

JIMMIEBOY AND THE BROTHERS CLAUS.

"This is a poor sick little fellow we are going to see first," he said. "He wanted a set of choo-choo cars, but we can't give them to him because the only set we have is for you, Jimmieboy. Your application came in before his did. I hope he won't be disappointed, though I am afraid he will be. A fish-pond isn't half so much fun as a set of choo-choo cars."

"That's so," said Jimmieboy. "But, Mr. Marmy, perhaps, if it's going to make him feel real bad not to get them—maybe—perhaps you might let him have the cars. I don't want them too much." This wasn't quite true, but Jimmieboy, somehow or other, didn't like to think of the little sick boy waking up on Christmas day and not finding what he wanted. "You know, I have one engine and a coal car left of my old set, and I guess maybe, perhaps, I can make them do," he added.

Marmy gave the little fellow an affectionate squeeze, and said: "Well, if you really feel that way, maybe we had better leave the cars there. Eh, Santa?"

"Maybe, perhaps," said Santa.

And it so happened; and although he could not tell exactly why, Jimmieboy felt happier after leaving the cars at the little sick boy's house than he ever thought he could be.

"Now, Jimmieboy," said Santa, as Marmy took the reins and they drove off again, "while Marmy and I are attending to the hotels and flat-houses, we want you to take that brown bag and go down the chimney of the orphan asylum, and leave one toy for each little child there. There are about a hundred little orphans to be provided for."

"What's orphans?" asked Jimmieboy.

"Orphans? Why, they are poor little boys and girls without any papas and mammas, and they all have to live together in one big house. You'll see 'em fast asleep in their little white cots when you get down the chimney, and you must be very careful not to wake them up."

"I'll try not to," said Jimmieboy, softly, a lump growing up in his throat as he thought of the poor children who had no parents. "And I'll make sure they all get something, too."

"That's right," said Marmy. "And here's where they live. You take the bag now, and we'll let you down easy, and when we get through, we'll come back for you."

So Jimmieboy shouldered the bag full of toys, and was lowered through the chimney into the room where the orphans were sleeping. He was surprised to find how light the bag was, and he was almost afraid there would not be enough toys to go around; but there were, as he found out in a moment. There were more than enough by at least a dozen of the most beautiful toys he had ever seen—just the very things he would most have liked to have himself.

"I just guess I'll give 'em one of these things apiece, and keep the extra ones, and maybe perhaps they'll be for me," he said.

So he arranged the toys quietly under the stockings that hung at the foot of the little white beds, stuffing the stockings themselves with candies

JIMMIEBOY IN THE ORPHAN ASYLUM.

and apples and raisins and other delicious things to eat, and then sat down by the fire-place to await the return of Santa Claus and Santa's brother Marmy. As he sat there he looked around the dimly lighted room, and saw the poor thin white faces of the little sleeping orphans, and his heart stirred with pity for their sad condition. Then he looked at the bag again, and saw the extra dozen toys that were so pleasing to him, and he wondered if it would make the orphans happier next morning if they should wake and find them there, too. At first he wasn't sure but that the orphans had enough; and then he thought of his own hamper full of dolls, and dogs, and tin soldiers, and cars, and blocks, at home, and he tried to imagine how much fun he could get out of a single toy, and he couldn't quite bring himself to believe that he could get much.

"One toy is great fun for an hour," he said to himself, "but for a year, dear me! I guess I won't keep them, after all. I'll just put them in the middle of the room, so that they'll find them in the morning, and maybe perhaps—— Hello!" he added, as he took the extra toys out of the bag: "they were for me, after all. They've got my name on 'em. Oh, dear! isn't it love—— I don't know, though. Seems to me I'd better leave them here, even if they are for me. I can get along without them because I have a papa to play with, and he's more fun than any toy I ever had; and mamma's better'n any doll baby or choo-choo car I ever saw. Yes, I will leave them."

And the little fellow was true to his purpose. He emptied the bag to the very last toy, and then, hearing the tinkling bells of Santa's sleigh on the roof again, he ran to the chimney, and was hauled up by his two new friends to the roof.

"Why, you've left everything except the bag!" cried Marmy, as Jimmieboy climbed into the sleigh.

"Yes," said Jimmieboy, with a little sigh; "everything."

"But the bag had all your things in it, and we haven't a toy or a sugar-plum left for you," said Santa.

"Never mind," said Jimmieboy. "I don't care much. I've had this ride with you, and—al—together I'm—pret--ty well—satis—fi——"

Here the little assistant to the Claus brothers, lulled by the jingling of the bells, fell asleep.

It was morning when he waked again—Christmas morning—and as he opened his eyes he found himself back in his little crib, pondering over the mysterious experiences of the night. His heart was strangely light and happy even for him, especially when he thought of the little orphan children, and tried to imagine their happiness on waking and finding the extra toys—his toys—in addition to their own; and as he thought about it, his eyes wandered to the chimney-place, and an unexpected sight met his gaze, for there stood the much-wished-for velocipede, and grouped around it on the floor were a beautiful set of choo-choo cars exactly like those he had left with the sick boy, and a duplicate of every one of the extra toys he had left at the asylum for the orphans.

"They must have been playing a joke on me," he cried, in delighted tones, as he sprang out of bed and rushed over to where the toys lay. "I do believe they left them here while I was in the asylum. The—dear—old—things!"

And then Jimmieboy was able to measure the delight of the orphan children and the little sufferer by comparing it with his own; and when he went to bed that night, he whispered in his mamma's ear that he didn't know for sure, but he thought that if the orphans only had a papa and a mamma like his, they would certainly be the happiest little children in all the world.

II

THE DWARF AND THE DUDE GIANT.

THE day had not yet dawned, but Jimmieboy was awake - wide awake. So wide awake was he, indeed, that the small bed in which he had passed the night was not broad enough by some ten or twelve feet to accommodate the breadth of his wakefulness, and he had in consequence crawled over into his father's bed, seated himself as nearly upon his father's neck as was possible, and was vociferously demanding a story.

"Oh, wait a little while, Jimmieboy," said his father, wearily. "I'm sound asleep—can't you see?"

"Tell a story," said Jimmieboy, poking his thumbs into his father's half closed eyes.

The answer was a snore—not a real one, but one of those imitation snores that fathers of boys like Jimmieboy make use of on occasions of this sort, prompted no doubt by the maker's desire to convince a persistent enemy to sleep that his cause is hopeless, and of which the enemy is never to be convinced.

"Tell a story about a Giant," insisted Jimmieboy, a suggestion of tears in his voice.

"Oh, well," returned the sleepy father, sitting up and rubbing his eyes vigorously in a vain effort to get all the sleepiness out of them. "If you must have it, you must have it, so here goes. Let's see—a story of a Giant or of a Dwarf?"

"Both," said Jimmieboy, placidly.

"Dear me!" cried his father. "I wish I'd kept quiet about the Dwarf. Well, once upon a time there was a Giant."

"And a Dwarf, too," put in Jimmieboy, who did not intend to be cheated out of a half of the story.

"Yes. And a Dwarf, too," said the other with a nod. "The Giant was a Dude Giant, who cared more for his hats than he did for anything else in the world. It was quite natural, too, that he should, for he had a finer chance to show them off than most people have, because he had no less than four heads, which is very remarkable for a Dude Giant, because dudes who are not

giants very rarely have even one head worth
mentioning. Hats were about the only things
the Dude Giant cared for at all. He used to buy
every style of head-gear he could find, and it
took almost all of the salary he received at the
Museum where he was on exhibition to pay for
them; but he was particularly fond of silk hats.
Of these he had twenty-eight; four for each day
of the week, those for Sunday being especially
handsome and costly.

"Now it happened that in the same exhibition
with the Dude Giant there was a Dwarf named
Tiny W. Littlejohn— W standing for Wee,
which was his middle name. He was a very
good-natured fellow, Tiny was, and as far as he
knew he hadn't an enemy in the world. He was
so very nice that everybody who came to the exhibition brought him cream cakes, and picture
books, and roller skates, and other beautiful
things, and nobody ever thought of going away
without buying his photograph, paying him
twenty-five cents extra for the ones with his
autograph on, which his mother wrote for him.
In this way the Dwarf soon grew to be a million-
aire, while the Dude Giant squandered all he
had on riotous hats, and so remained as poor as
when he started. For a long time everything

went smoothly at the Exhibition. There were no jealousies or quarrels of any sort, except between the Glass Eater and the man who made Glass Steamboats, and that was smoothed over in a very short time by the Glass Eater saying that the Glass-blower made the finest crystal pies he had ever tasted. But contentment and peace could not last forever in an establishment where one attraction was growing richer and richer every day as the Dwarf was, while another, the Dude Giant, was no better off than the day he joined the show, and when finally the Dwarf began to come every morning in a cab of his own, drawn by a magnificent gray horse with a banged tail, and to dress better even than the proprietor of the Museum himself, the Dude Giant became very envious, and when the Dude Giant gets envious he is a very disagreeable person. For instance, when no one was looking he would make horrible faces at Tiny, contorting his four mouths and noses and eight cheeks all at once in a very terrifying manner, and when he'd look cross-eyed at the Dwarf with all eight of his eyes poor Tiny would get so nervous that he would try to eat the roller skates and picture books, instead of the cream cakes people brought him, and on one occasion he broke two of his prettiest teeth doing it, which marred his personal appearance very much.

"Tiny stood it as long as he could, and then he complained to his friend, the Whirlwind, about it, and the Whirlwind, who was a very sensible sort of a fellow, advised him not to mind it. It was only jealousy, he said, that led the Dude Giant to behave that way, and if Tiny had not been more successful than Forepate—as the Dude Giant was called—Forepate wouldn't have been jealous, so that his very jealousy was an acknowledgment of inferiority. So Tiny made up his mind he wouldn't pay any attention to the Dude Giant at all, but would go right ahead minding his own business and making all the money he could.

"This made Forepate all the more angry, and finally he resolved to get even with the Dwarf in some other way than by making grimaces at him. Now, it happened that Forepate's place was over by a window directly opposite to where the Dwarf sat, and so, to get near enough to Tiny to put his scheme against him into execution, he complained to the manager that there was a terrible draft from the window, and added that unless he could sit on the other side of the room he was certain he'd catch cold in three of his heads anyhow, if not in all of them.

"'Very well,' said the manager. 'Where do you wish to sit?'

"'You might put me next to Littlejohn, over there,' said the head with red hair.

"'But,' said the manager, 'what shall we do with that stuffed owl with the unicorn's horns?'

"'Put him by the window,' said another of the Dude Giant's heads.

"'Yes,' said the third head. 'No draft in all the world could give a stuffed owl a cold.'

"'That's so,' replied the manager. 'We'll make the change right off.'

"And then the change was made, though Tiny did not like it very much.

"To disarm all suspicion, the Dude Giant was very affable to the Dwarf for a whole week, and to see him talking to Tiny no one would have suspected that he hated him so, which shows how horribly crafty he was. Finally the hour for his revenge arrived. It was Monday morning, and Forepate and Tiny had taken their places as usual, when, observing that no one was looking, Forepate took his biggest beaver hat and put it over Tiny, completely hiding him from view. Poor Tiny was speechless with rage, and so could not cry out. Forepate kept him under his hat all day, and whenever any one asked where Littlejohn was, one of his heads would say, 'Alas! Poor Tiny, he has mysteriously disappeared!' And another head would shake itself and say 'Somebody must have left the door open and the wind must have whisked the dear little fellow out into the cold, cold world.' Then the other two heads would blubber, at which the Dude Giant would take out his handkerchiefs and wipe his eight eyes and shake all over as if he were inconsolable, and Tiny, overhearing it all, grew more and more speechless with indignation.

"That night, of course, Forepate had to release him, and Tiny hurried away fairly howling with anger. When he arrived at home he told his mother how he had been treated and how he had been done out of a whole day's cream cakes and picture books and roller skates, and she advised him to go at once to the Whirlwind and confide his woe to him, which he did.

"'Forepate ought to be ashamed of himself,' said the Whirlwind, when Tiny had told' his story.

"'But he never does what he ought to do unless somebody makes him,' said Tiny, ruefully.

'Can't we do something to make him ashamed of himself?'

" 'Well, I'll see,' said the Whirlwind, with a shake of his head that meant that he intended to do something. 'What does the Dude Giant do with himself on Sundays?'

" 'Shows off his best hats on Fifth avenue," returned the Dwarf.

" 'Very well then, I have it,' said the Whirlwind. 'Next Sunday, Tiny, we'll have our revenge on Forepate. You stand on one of the stoops at the corner of Fifth avenue and Thirty-fourth street at midday, and you'll see a sight that will make you happy for the rest of your days.'

"So, on the following Sunday the Dwarf climbed up on one of the front stoops on Fifth avenue, near Thirty-fourth street, and waited. He hadn't been there long when he saw Forepate striding down the avenue dressed in his best clothes, and wearing upon his heads four truly magnificent beavers, which he had just received from London, and of which he was justly proud.

" 'I wonder where the Whirlwind is,' thought the Dwarf, looking anxiously up and down the avenue for his avenger. 'I do hope he won't fail."

"Hardly were the words out of his mouth when Forepate reached the crossing of Thirty-fourth street, and just as he stepped from the walk into the street, bzoo! along came the Whirlwind, and off went Forepate's treasured hats. One hat flew madly up Fifth avenue. A second rolled swiftly down Fifth avenue. A third tripped merrily along East Thirty-fourth street, while the fourth sailed joyously into the air, struck a lamp-post, and then plunged along West Thirty-fourth street. And then! Dear me! What a terrible thing happened! It was perfectly awful—simply dreadful!"

"Hurry up and tell it," said Jimmieboy, jumping up and down with anxiety to hear what happened next.

"Then," said his papa, "when the Dude Giant saw his beloved hats flying in every direction he howled aloud with every one of his four voices, and craned each of his necks in the direction in which it's hat had flown.

"Then the head with the auburn hair demanded that the Giant should immediately run up Fifth avenue to recover it's lost beaver, and the giant started, but hardly had he gone a step when the head with the black hair cried out:

"'No! Down Fifth avenue after my hat.'

"'Not at all!' shrieked the head without any hair. 'Go east after mine.'

"'Well, I guess not!' roared the head that had curly hair. 'He's going west after mine.'

"Meanwhile the Giant had come to a standstill. He couldn't run in any direction until his heads had agreed as to which way he should go, and all this time the beautiful hats were getting farther and farther away, and the heads more frantic than ever. For five full minutes they quarreled thus among themselves, turning now and then to peer weepingly after their beloved silk hats, and finally, with a supreme effort, each endeavored to force the Giant in the direction it wished him to go, with the result that poor Forepate was torn to pieces, and fell dead in the middle of the street."

Here papa paused and closed his eyes for a minute.

"Is that all?" queried Jimmieboy.

"Yes—I believe that's all. The Dude Giant was dead and the Dwarf was avenged."

"And what became of Tiny?" asked Jimmieboy.

"Oh, Tiny," said his father, "Tiny—he—he laughed so heartily at the Dude Giant's mishap that he loosened the impediment to his growth.—"

"The what?" asked Jimmieboy, to whom words like impediment were rather strange.

"Why, the bone that kept him from growing," explained the story teller. "He loosened that and began to grow again, and inside of two weeks he was as handsome a six-footer as you ever saw, and as he had made a million and a half of dollars he resigned from the Exhibition and settled down in Europe for a number of years, had himself made a Grand Duke, and then came back to New York and got married, and lived happy ever after."

And then, as the getting-up bell rang down stairs, Jimmieboy thanked his father for the story and went into the nursery to dress for breakfast.

III.

JIMMIEBOY'S DREAM POETRY.

IF there is anything in the world that Jimmie-boy likes better than custard and choo-choo cars, it is to snuggle down in his papa's lap about bedtime and pretend to keep awake. It doesn't matter at all how tired he is, or how late bedtime may on special occasions be delayed, he is never ready to be undressed and "filed away for the night," as his Uncle Periwinkle puts it.

It was just this way the other night. He was as sleepy as he possibly could be. The sandman had left enough sand in his eyes, or so it seemed to Jimmieboy, to start a respectable sea-beach, and he really felt as if all he needed to make a summer resort of himself was a big hotel, a band of music, and an ocean. But in spite of all this he didn't want to go to bed, and he had

apparently made up his mind that he was n't going to want to go to bed for some time to come;
and as his papa was in an unusually indulgent
mood, the little fellow was permitted to nestle up
close under his left arm and sit there on his lap in
the library after dinner, while his mamma read
aloud an article in one of the magazines on the
subject of dream poetry.

It was a very interesting article, Jimmieboy
thought. The idea of anybody's writing poetry
while asleep struck him as being very comical,
and he laughed several times in a sleepy sort of
way, and then all of a sudden he thought, "Why,
if other people can do it, why can't I?"

"Why?" he answered—he was quite fond of
asking himself questions and then answering
them—"why? Because you can't write at all.
You don't know an H from a D, unless there's
a Horse in the picture with the H, and a Donkey
with the D. That's why."

"True; but that's only when I'm awake."

"Try it and see," whispered the Pencil in his
papa's vest pocket. "I'll help, and maybe our
old friend the Scratch Pad will help too."

"That's a good idea," said Jimmieboy, taking
the Pencil out of his papa's pocket, and assisting
it to climb down to the floor, so that it could run

over to the desk and tell the Scratch Pad it was
wanted

"Don't you lose my pencil," said papa.

"No, I won't," replied Jimmieboy, his eyes following the Pencil in its rather winding course
about the room to where the desk stood.

"I have to keep out of sight, you know, Jimmieboy," the Pencil said, in a low tone of voice,
"Because if I didn't, and your papa saw me
walking off, he'd grab hold of me and put me
back in his pocket again."

Suddenly the Pencil disappeared over by the
waste-basket, and then Jimmieboy heard him
calling, in a loud whisper: "Hi! Pad! Paddy!
Pad-dee!"

"What's wanted?" answered the Pad, crawling over the edge of the desk and peering down
at the Pencil, who was by this time hallooing
himself hoarse.

"Jimmieboy and I are going to write some
dream poetry, and we want you to help," said the
Pencil.

"Oh, I'm not sleepy," said the Pad.

"Neither am I," returned the Pencil. "But
that needn't make any difference. Jimmieboy
does the sleeping and dreaming, and you and I
do the rest."

"Oh, that's it, eh? Well, then, I don't mind; but—er—how am I ever going to get down there?" asked the Pad. "It's a pretty big jump."

"That's so," answered the Pencil. "I wouldn't try jumping. Can't the Twine help you?"

"No. He's all used up."

"Then I have it," said the Pencil. "Put a little

ARM IN ARM THEY TIPTOED SOFTLY ACROSS THE ROOM.

mucilage on your back and slide down. The mucilage will keep you from going too fast."

"Good scheme," said the Pad, putting the Pencil's suggestion into practice, and finding that it worked beautifully, even if it did make him feel uncomfortably sticky

And then, arm in arm, they tip-toed softly across the room and climbed up into Jimmieboy's lap. So quietly did they go that neither Jimmieboy's mamma, nor his papa noticed them at all, as they might have had the conspirators been noisy, although mamma was reading and papa's head was thrown back, so that his eyes rested on the picture moulding.

"Here we are, Jimmieboy," said the Pad. "Pen here tells me you're going to try a little dream poetry."

"Yes," said Jimmieboy. "I am, if you two will help."

"Count on us," said the Pencil. "What do you do first?"

"I don't exactly know," said Jimmieboy. "But I rather think I take Pencil in my hand, Pad in my lap, and fall asleep."

"All right," said the Pad, lying flat on his back. "I'm ready."

"So am I," put in the Pencil, settling down between two of Jimmieboy's fingers.

"All aboard for sleep," said Jimmieboy, with a smile, and then he fell into a doze. In about two minutes he opened his eyes again, and found both Pad and Pencil in a great state of excitement.

"Did I write anything?" asked Jimmieboy, in an excited whisper.

"Yes," said the Pad. "You just covered me up with a senseless mass of words. This isn't any fun."

"No," said the Pencil. "It's all nonsense. Just see here what you've got."

Jimmieboy looked anxiously at the Pad, and this is what he saw:

<pre>
I   seen   since,
            memory's   wrong,
      They both   dressed
                  couple walked

      And straightway change
                  upstairs with me,
                  " I think it's
      " If that's the case,"

                  catch the early   in."
                        to leave the shop,
                        for it's pla
                        Polypop.

            two weeks yesterday."
            haven't uttered
      Oh, Polypop, I
                  ersnee, " See here,

      He didn't pay
                  moon was shining bright.
      To see the
            Polypop came down
</pre>

"Dear me!" he said. "Why, that doesn't mean anything, does it?"

JIMMIEBOY FINDS NOTHING BUT DREAM-WRITING
ON THE PAD.

"No. There isn't much in dream poetry, I guess," said the Pad. "I'm going back home. Good-by.

" "Oh, don't go," said the Pencil.   "Let's try it
again—just once more.   Eh?"

"Very well," returned the Pad, good-natured-
ly, tearing off one of his leaves. "Go ahead, Jimmieboy."

And Jimmieboy dozed off again.

"Wake up, wake up!" cried the Pencil in
about three minutes.   "We've got something
this time."

But they were all disappointed, for, when they
looked, all that they could see was this:

<pre>
            have not   them
       And if my   not
                   were   in chintz ;
       With that the   along ;

                              your vest."
       For you to go
       Replied   best,
                       the Snickersnee,

       And   tra
         I hadn't time
       "My reason   in ;
       "I know it," said the

       Since
       You   one small cheer,
                       say,
       Then quoth the Snick
</pre>

his fee.

And as the

Snickersnee,

The one night,

"Rubbish!" said the Pad, indignantly. "There's two leaves of myself wasted now on your old dream poetry. I think that's enough. I'm off. Good-by."

"Don't be hasty, Pad," retorted the Pencil. "That's a great deal better than the other. Why, there's one part there with all the lines beginning with capitals, and when that happens it's generally a sign that there's poetry around."

"There isn't much there, though," said Jimmieboy, a little disappointed by the result. "I guess Pad's right. We'd better give it up."

"Not yet," pleaded the Pencil. "There's luck in odd numbers, you know. Let's try it just once more."

"Shall we, Jimmieboy?" asked the Pad.

"Yes. Let's," assented Jimmieboy, as he dropped off to sleep for the third time.

This time he must have slept five minutes. When he opened his eyes he saw the Pencil staring blankly at the Pad, on which was written nothing more than this curious looking formula:

$$\frac{\begin{array}{c}2\\2\end{array}}{4}$$

"How aggravating!" said Jimmieboy.

"Abominable!" ejaculated the Pad.

"I believe it's a key to what has gone before," said the Pencil, shaking his rubber wisely. "Two and two make four—two and two make four. Ah! I know. You've got to put two and two together to make four. If we put those two leaves of nonsensical words together, maybe we'll have a poem. Let's try."

"It'll use me up, I'm afraid," sighed the Pad.

"Oh, no. It won't take more than a half of you," said the Pencil, putting the two leaves on which Jimmieboy had first written together.

"It looks like a poem," he said, when he had fitted the two together. "Let's see how it reads.

> "I have not seen them since,
> And if my memory's not wrong,
> They both were dressed in chintz,
> With that the couple walked along;"

"That doesn't mean a blessed thing," said the Pad.

"It's nonsense," said Jimmieboy.

"Just wait!" said the Pencil, beginning to read again:

And straightway change your vest."
For you to go upstairs with me,
Replied, "I think it's best
"If that's the case," the Snickersnee

And catch the early train."
I hadn't time to leave the shop
"My reason for it's plain;
"I know it," said the Polypop;

Since two weeks yesterday."
You haven't uttered one small cheer
Oh, Polypop, I say,
Then quoth the Snickersnee, "See here,

He didn't pay his fee.
And as the moon was shining bright,
To see the Snickersnee,
The Polypop came down one night

"Ho!" jeered the Pad. "That's elegant poetry, that is. You might get paid five cents a mile for stuff like that, if you wanted to sell it and had luck."

"I don't care," said the Pencil. "It rhymes well."

"Oh, I know what's the matter," said Jimmieboy, gleefully. "Why, of course it's poetry. Read it upside down, and it's all right. It's dream poetry, and dreams always go the other way. Why, it's fine. Just listen:

"The Polypop came down one night
　　To see the Snickersnee,
And, as the moon was shining bright,
　　He didn't pay his fee."

"That is good," said the Pad. "Let me say the
next:

"Then, quoth the Snickersnee, 'See here,
　　Oh, Polypop, I say,
You have not uttered one small cheer
　　Since two weeks yesterday.'"

"I thought it would come out right," said the
Pencil. "The next two verses are particularly
good, too:

"'I know it,' said the Polypop;
　　'My reason for it's plain;
I hadn't time to leave the shop
　　And catch the early train.'

"'If that's the case,' the Snickersnee
　　Replied, 'I think it's best
For you to go upstairs with me,
　　And straightway change your vest.'"

"Now altogether," cried the Pad, enthusiastic-
ally. "One, two, three!" And then they all
recited:

"With that the couple walked along;
　　They both were dressed in chintz;
And if my memory's not wrong,
　　I have not seen them since."

"Hooray!" cried Jimmieboy, as they finished
—so loudly that it nearly deafened the Pad,
which jumped from his lap and scurried back to
the table as fast as it could go.

"What's that cheer for?" asked papa, looking
down into Jimmieboy's face, and grabbing the
Pencil, which was on the point of falling to the
floor.

"It's for Dream Poetry," murmured Jimmieboy, getting drowsy again. "I've just dreamed
a lot. It's on the Pad."

"Indeed!" said papa, with a sly wink at mamma. "Let's get the Pad and read it."

The little fellow straightened up and ran
across to the desk, and, grasping the Pad firmly
in his hands, handed it to his father to read.

"H'm!" said papa, staring at the leaf before
him. "Blank verse."

"Read it," said Jimmieboy.

"I cant' to-night, my boy," he answered. "My
eyes are too weak for me to see dream writing."

For between you and me that was the only kind
of writing there was on that Pad.

IV.

A SUBTERRANEAN MUTINY.

IT seemed rather strange that it should have been left there, and yet Jimmieboy was glad that in grading his papa's tennis-court the men had left that bit of flat rock to show up on the surface of the lawn. It had afforded him no end of pleasure since he had first discovered it. As a make-believe island in a raging sea of grass, he had often used it to be cast away upon, but chiefly had he employed it as a vantage ground from which to watch his father and his father's friends at their games of tennis. The rock was just about large enough for the boy to sit upon and pretend that he was umpire, or, as his father said, mascot for his father's opponents, and it rarely happened that a game of tennis was played upon the court that was not witnessed by Jimmieboy seated upon his rocky coigne.

The strangest experience that Jimmieboy ever

had with this bit of stone, however, was one
warm afternoon last summer. It was at the
drowsy period of the day. The tennis players
were indulging in a game, which, to the little on-
looker, was unusually dull, and he was on the
point of starting off in pursuit of something, it
mattered not what, so long as it was interesting
enough to keep him awake, when he observed a
most peculiar thing about the flat stone. It had
unquestionably become transparent! Jimmieboy
could see through it, and what he saw was of
most unexpected quality.

"Dear me!" he ejaculated, "how very queer.
This rock is made of glass."

Then he peered down through it, and saw a
beautiful marble staircase running down into
the earth, at the foot of which was a great door
that looked as though it was made of silver, and
the key was of gold. At the sides of the staircase, hanging upon the walls, were pictures of
strange little men and women, but unlike the
men and women in other pictures, they moved
about, and talked, and romped, and seemed to
enjoy themselves hugely. Great pictures were
they indeed to Jimmieboy's mind, because they
were constantly changing, like the designs in
his kaleidoscope.

"I must get down there," he said, softly, to himself. "But how?"

As he spoke the door at the foot of the steps opened, and a small creature, for all the world like the goblin in Jimmieboy's fairy book, poked his head out. The goblin looked all about him, and then turning his eyes upward until they met those of the boy, he cried out:

"Hullo! Are you the toy peddler?"

"No," replied Jimmieboy.

"Then you are the milk broker, or the potato merchant, and we don't want any milk or any potatoes."

The goblin slammed the door when he had said this, and with such a bang that all the little people in the pictures ran to the edge of the frame and peered out to see what was the matter. One poor little fellow, who had been tending sheep in a picture half-way up the stairs, leaned out so far that he lost his balance and tumbled out head over heels. The sheep scampered over the hill and disappeared in the background of the painting.

"Poor little shepherd boy!" said Jimmieboy. "I hope you are not hurt!"

The shepherd boy looked up gratefully at the speaker, and said he wasn't, except in his feelings.

"Is there any way for me to get in there?" asked Jimmieboy.

"No, sir," said the shepherd boy. "That is, not all of you. Part of you can come in."

"Ho!" said Jimmieboy. "I can't divide myself up."

"Yes, you can," returned the shepherd boy. "It's easy enough, when you know how, but I suppose you don't know how, not having studied arithmetic. You can't even add, much less divide."

"Maybe you can tell me how," said Jimmieboy.

"Certainly, I can," said the shepherd boy. "The part of you that can come in is your eye, and your ear, and your voice. All the rest of you must stay out."

"But how do I get 'em in?" asked Jimmieboy.

"They are in now," said the other. "You can see me, you can hear me, and I can hear you."

"But I can't see what's beyond that door."

"Oh, we'll fix that," said the little shepherd. "I'll knock on the door, and when it is opened you can tell the goblin that you want to see what he's got, and he'll show it all to you if you tell him that your father is the man who didn't blast the rock out."

The shepherd boy then went softly down the stairs, knocked on the door, and before it was opened had flown back to his duties in the picture. Then, as he had intimated, the goblin opened the door again, and poking his head out as before, cried:

"Is that you, milk broker?"

"No," answered Jimmieboy. "I am the son of the man who didn't blast away the flat rock, and my eye and my ear and my voice want to come in."

"Why, certainly," said the goblin, throwing the door wide open. "I didn't know you were you. Let 'em walk right in."

Jimmieboy was about to say that he didn't know how his eye or his ear or his voice could walk anywhere, but he was prevented from so doing by the sudden disappearance of the staircase, and the substitution therefor of a huge room, the splendor of which was so great that it for a moment dazzled his eyes.

"Who comes here?" said a voice in the corner of the room.

"The eye and the ear and the voice of the son of the man who did not blast the flat stone," observed the goblin, and then Jimmieboy perceived, seated upon a lustrous golden throne,

a shriveled-up dwarf, who looked as if he might
be a thousand years old, but who, to judge from
the crown he wore upon his head, was a king.

The dwarf was clad in garments of the richest
texture, and his person was luminous with jewels
of the rarest sort. As the goblin announced the
visitor the king rose up, and descending from
the throne, made a courtly bow to Jimmieboy.

"Thrice welcome, O son of the man who did
not blast the flat rock," he said. "It is only fit-
ting that one who owes so much to the father
should welcome the eye and the ear and the
voice of the son, for know, O boy, that I am the
lord of the Undergroundies whose kingdom
would have been shattered but for your father's
kindly act in sparing it."

"I suppose that blasting the rock would have
spoiled all this," said Jimmieboy's voice, as his
eye took in the royal magnificence of the place,
while to his ears came strains of soft and sweet
music. "It would have been dreadful!"

"Much more dreadful than you imagine," replied the little king. "It would have worked
damage that a life-time could not have repaired."

Then the king turned to a tall, pale creature
in black who sat writing at a mahogany table in
one corner of the throne room, and commanded

him to recite into Jimmieboy's ear how dreadful it would have been.

"Compose, O laureate," he said to the tall, pale creature, "compose a song in which the dire effects of such a blast are fully set forth."

The laureate rose from his seat, and bowing low before the king and Jimmieboy's eye, began his song, which ran in this wise:

> "A half a pound of dynamite
>   Set in that smooth, flat stone,
>   Our palace would quite out of signt
>   Most certainly have blown.
>
> "It would have blown our window-panes
>   To high Gibraltar's ledge,
>   And all our streets and country lanes
>   It would have set on edge.
>
> "It would have knocked our royal king
>   As far up as the moon:
>   Beyond the reach of anything—
>   Beyond the best balloon.
>
> "It would have taken all our pears,
>   Our candy and our toys,
>   And hurled them where the polar bears
>   Indulge in horrid noise.
>
> "It would have spoiled the music-box,
>   And ruined all our books—
>   Knocked holes in all our woolen socks,
>   And ruined thus their looks.

> "'Twould have destroyed our chandeliers,
>   To dough turned all our pie;
> And, worst of all, my little dears,
>   It would have injured I."

"Is that dreadful enough?" asked t' e laureate, turning to the king.

"It suits me," said the king. "But perhaps our friend Jimmieboy would like to have it made a little more dreadful."

"In that case," said the laureate, "I can compose a few more verses in which the blast makes the tennis-court over us cave in and bury all the cake and jam we have in the larder, or if he thinks that too much to sacrifice, and would like a little pleasure mixed in with the terribleness, the cod-liver oil bottle might be destroyed."

"I wouldn't spoil the cake and jam," said Jimmieboy's voice, in reply to this. "But the cod-liver oil might go."

"Very well," said the laureate, and then he bowed low again and sang:

> "But there is balm for our annoy,
>   For next the blast doth spoil
> Six hundred quarts—O joy! O joy!—
>   Of vile cod   ver oil."

"I should think you would have liked that," said Jimmieboy's voice.

"I would have," said the king, "because you know the law of this country requires the king to consume a bottle of cod-liver oil every day, and if the bottles were all broken, perhaps the law, too, would have been crushed out of existence. But, after all, I'd rather be king with cod-liver oil than have my kingdom ruined and do without it. How would you like to see our gardens?"

"Very much," said Jimmieboy. "I'm fond of flowers."

The king laughed.

"What a droll idea," he said, turning to the laureate. "The idea of flowers growing in gardens! Write me a rhyme on the drollness of the idea."

The laureate sighed. It was evident that he was getting tired of composing verses to order.

"I hear and obey," he replied, shortly, and then he recited as follows:

> "To think of wasting any time
>   In raising flowers, I think,
> Is worse than writing nonsense-rhyme,
>   Or frying purple ink.

> "It's queerer really than the act
>   Of painting sword-fish green ;
> Or sailing down a cataract
>   To please a magazine.

> "Indeed, it really seems to me,
> Who now am very old,
> The drollest bit of drollery
> That ever has been drolled."

"But what do you raise in your gardens?" asked Jimmieboy, as the laureate completed his composition.

"Nothing, of course," said the king. "What's a garden for, anyhow? Pleasure, isn't it?"

"Yes," said Jimmeboy's voice, "but——"

"There isn't any but about it," said the king. "If a garden is for pleasure it must not be worked in. Business and pleasure are two very different things, and you cannot raise flowers without working."

"But how do you get pleasure out of a garden when you don't raise anything in it?"

"Aren't you dull!" ejaculated the king. "Write me a quatrain on his dullness, O laureate."

"Confound his dullness!" muttered the laureate. "I'm rapidly wearing out, poetizing about this boy." Then he added, aloud: "Certainly, your majesty. Here it is:

> "He is the very dullest lad
> I've seen in all my life;
> For dullness he is quite as bad
> As any oyster-knife."

"Is that all?" asked the king, with a frown.

"I'm afraid four lines is as many as I can squeeze into a quatrain," said the laureate, returning the frown with interest.

"Then tell this young man's ear, sirrah, how it comes that we get pleasure out of a garden in which nothing grows."

"If I must—I suppose I must," growled the laureate; and then he recited:

> "The plan is thus, O little wit,
>   You'll see it in a minute;
> We get our pleasures out of it,
>   Because there's none within it."

"That is very poor poetry, Laury!" snapped the king.

"If you don't like it, don't take it," retorted the laureate. "I'm tired of this business, anyhow."

"And what, pray," cried the king, striding angrily forward to the mutinous poet, "what are you going to do about it?"

"I'm going to get up a revolution," retorted the laureate, shaking his quill pen fiercely at the king. "If I go to the people to-morrow, and promise not to write any more poetry, they'll all be so grateful they'll make me king, and set you to work wheeling coal in the mines for the mortals."

The king's face grew so dark with anger as the laureate spoke that Jimmieboy's eye could hardly see two inches before itself, and in haste the little fellow withdrew it from the scene. What happened next he never knew, but that missiles were thrown by the quarreling king and poet he was certain, for there was a tremendous shout, and something just tipped the end of his ear and went whizzing by, and rubbing his eyes, the boy looked about him, and discovered that he was still lying face downward upon the flat rock, but it was no longer transparent.

Off in the bushes directly back of him was his father, looking for a tennis ball. This, some people say, is the object that whizzed past Jimmieboy's ear, but to this day the little fellow believes that it was nothing less than the king's crown, which that worthy monarch had hurled at the laureate, that did this.

For my part I take sides with neither, for, as a matter of fact, I know nothing about it.

V.

JIMMIEBOY IN THE LIBRARY.

"I'M going to sit in this comfor'ble arm-chair by
the fire," said Jimmieboy, climbing up into
the capacious easy-chair in his father's library,
and settling down upon its soft cushioned seat.
"I've had my supper, and it was all of cold
things, and I think I ought to get 'em warmed
up before I go to bed."

"Very well," said his papa. "Only be careful,
and keep your feet awake. It wouldn't be comfortable if your feet should go to sleep just about
the time your mamma wanted you to go to bed.
I'd have to carry you up stairs, if that should
happen, and the doctor says if I carry you much
longer I'll have a back like a dromedary."

"Oh, that would be lovely!" said Jimmieboy.
"I'd just like to see you with two humps on your

back—one for me, and one for my little brother."

"Dear me!" said a gruff voice at Jimmieboy's side—"Dear me! The idea of a boy of your age, with two sets of alphabet picture blocks and a dictionary right in the house, not knowing that a dromedary has only one hump! Ridiculous! Next thing you'll be trying to say that the one-eyed catteraugus has two eyes."

Jimmieboy leaned over the arm of the chair to see who it could be that spoke. It wasn't his father, that much was certain, because his father had often said that it wasn't possible to do more than three things at once, and he was now doing that many—smoking a cigar, reading a book, and playing with the locket on the end of his watch-chain.

"Who are you, anyhow?" said Jimmieboy, as he peered over the arm, and saw nothing but the Dictionary.

"I'm myself—that's who," was the answer, and then Jimmieboy was interested to see that it was nothing less than the Dictionary itself that had addressed him. "You ought to be more careful about the way you talk," added the Dictionary. "Your diction is airy without being dictionary, if you know what that means, which you don't, as the Rose remarked to the Cauliflower, when the Cauliflower said he'd be a finer Rose than the Rose if he smelled as sweet."

"I'm very sorry," Jimmieboy replied, meekly, "I forgot that the dromedary only had one hump."

"I don't believe you'd know a dromedary from a milk dairy if they both stood before you," retorted the Dictionary. "Now would you?"

"Yes, I think I would," said Jimmieboy. "The milk dairy would have cream in bottles in its windows, and the dromedary wouldn't."

"Ah, but you don't know why!" sang the Dictionary. "You don't even begin to know why the dromedary wouldn't have cream in bottles in its windows."

"No," said Jimmieboy, "I don't. Why wouldn't he?"

"Because he has no windows," laughed the Dictionary; "and between you and me, that's one of the respects in which the dromedary is like a base-drum—there isn't a solitary window in either of 'em."

"You know a terrible lot, don't you?" said Jimmieboy, patronizingly.

"Terrible isn't the word. I'm simply hideously learned," said the Dictionary. "Why, I've been called a vocabulary, I know so many words."

JIMMIEBOY IN THE LIBRARY.   63

"I wish you'd tell me all you know," said
Jimmieboy, resting his elbows on the arms of
the chair, and putting his chin on the palms of
his two hands. "I'd like to know more than papa
does—just for once. Do you know enough to
tell me anything he doesn't know?"

"Do I?" laughed the Dictionary. "Well, don't
I? Rather. Why, I'm telling him things all the
time. He came and asked me the other night
what raucous meant, and how to spell macrobi-
otic."

"And did you really know?" asked Jimmieboy,
full of admiration for this wonderful creature.

"Yes: and a good deal more besides. Why, if
he had asked me, I could have told him what a
zygomatic zoophagan is; but he never asked
me. Queer, wasn't it?"

"Yes," said Jimmieboy. "What is one of those
things?"

"A zygomatic zoophagan? Why that's a—er
—let me see," said the Dictionary, turning
over his leaves. "I like to search myself pretty
thoroughly before I commit myself to a defini-
tion. A zygomatic zoophagan is a sort of cheeky
animal that eats other animals. You are one,
though I wouldn't brag about it if I were you.
You are an animal, and at times a very cheeky

animal, and I've seen you eat beef. That's what makes you a zygomatic zoophagan."

"Do I bite?" asked Jimmieboy, a little afraid of himself since he had learned what a fearful creature he was.

"Only at dinner-time, and unless you are very careless about it and eat too hastily you need not be afraid. Very few zygomatic zoophagans ever bite themselves. In fact, it never happened really but once that I know of. That was the time the zoophagan got the best of the eight-winged tallahassee. Ever hear about that?"

"No, I never did," said Jimmieboy. "How did it happen?"

"This way," said the Dictionary, as he stood up and made a bow to Jimmieboy. And then he recited these lines:

"THE CALIPEE AND THE ZOOPHAGAN."

"The yellow-faced Zoophagan
　　Was strolling near the sea,
When from the depths of ocean
Sprang forth that dread amp-hib-ian,
　　The mawkish Calipee.

"The Tallahassee bird sometimes
　　The Calipee is called.
His eyes are round and big as dimes,
He has eight wings, composes rhymes,
　　His head is very bald.

"Now if there are two creatures in
    This world who disagree—
Two creatures full of woe and sin—
They are the Zo-oph, pale and thin,
    And that bad Calipee.

"Whene'er they meet they're sure to fight,
    No matter where they are;
Nor do they stop by day or night,
Till one is beaten out of sight,
    Or safety seeks afar.

"And, sad to say, the Calipee
    Is stronger of the two;
And so he'd won the victory
At all times from his enemy,
    The slight and slender Zoo.

"But this time it went otherwise,
    For, so the story goes,
As yonder sun set in the skies,
The Calipee, to his surprise,
    Was whacked square on the nose.

"Which is the fatal, mortal part
    Of all the Calipees;
Much more important than the heart,
For life is certain to depart
    When Cali cannot sneeze.

"The world, surprised, asked 'How was it?
    How did he do it so?
Where did the Zoo get so much wit?
How did he learn so well to hit
    So fatally his foe?'

" ' 'Twas but his strategy,' then cried
　　The friends of little Zoo ;
'As Cali plunged, our hero shied,
Ran twenty feet off to one side,
　　And bit himself in two.

" ' And then, you see, the Calipee
　　Was certainly undone ;
The Zo-oph beat him easily,
As it must nearly always be
　　When there are two to one.'

"Rather a wonderful tale that," continued the Dictionary. "I don't know that I really believe it, though. It's too great a tale for any dog to wag, eh?"

"Yes," said Jimmieboy. "I don't think I believe it either. If the zoophagan bit himself in two, I should think he'd have died. I know I would."

"No, you wouldn't," said the Dictionary ; "because you couldn't. It isn't a question of would and could, but of wouldn't and couldn't. By-the-way, here's a chance for you to learn something. What's the longest letter in the alphabet?"

"They're all about the same, aren't they?" asked Jimmieboy.

"They look so, but they aren't. L is the longest. An English ell is forty-five inches long.

THE CALIPEE AND THE ZOOPHAGAN.

Here's another.   What letter does a Chinaman
wear on his head?"

"Double eye!" cried Jimmieboy.

"That's pretty good," said the Dictionary, with
an approving nod; "but you're wrong.   He
wears a Q.   And I'll tell you why a Q is like a
Chinaman.   Chinamen don't amount to a row of
beans, and a Q is nothing but a zero with a pig-
tail.   Do you know why they put A at the head
of the alphabet?"

"No."

"Because Alphabet begins with an A."

"Then why don't they put T at the end of it?"
asked Jimmieboy.

"They do," said the Dictionary.   "I-T—it."

Jimmieboy laughed to himself.   He had no
idea there was so much fun in the Dictionary.
"Tell me something more," he said.

"Let me see.   Oh, yes," said the Dictionary,
complacently.   "How's this?

> " 'Oh, what is a yak, sir?' the young man said ;
>   'I really much wish to hear.'
>   'A queer-looking cad with a bushy head,
>   A buffalo-robe all over him spread,
>   And whiskers upon his ear.'
>
> " 'And tell me, I pray,' said the boy in drab,
>   Just what's a Thelphusi-an?'
>   'A great big crab with nippers that nab

Whatever the owner desires to grab—
A crusty crustace-an."

"'I'm obliged,' said the boy, with a wide, wide
smirk,
As he slowly moved away.
'Will you tell me, sir, ere I go to work—
To toil till the night brings along its murk—
How high peanuts are to-day?'

"And I had to give in,
For I couldn't say;
And the boy, with a grin,
Moved off on his way."

"That was my own personal experience," said
the Dictionary. "The boy was a very mean boy,
too. He went about telling people that there
were a great many things I didn't know, which
was very true, only he never said what they
were, and his friends thought they were important things, like the meaning of sagacious-
ness, and how many jays are there in geranium,
and others. If he'd told 'em that it was things
like the price of peanuts, and how are the fish
biting to-day, and is your mother's seal-skin
sack plush or velvet, that I didn't know, they'd
not have thought it disgraceful. Oh, it was
awfully mean!"

"Particularly after you had told him what
those other things were," said Jimmieboy.

"Yes; but I got even with him. He came to me one day to find out what an episode was, and I told him it was a poem in hysterical hexameters, with a refrain repeated every eighteenth line, to be sung to slow music."

"And what happened?" asked Jimmieboy.

"He told his teacher that, and he was kept in for two months, and made to subtract two apples from one lunch every recess."

"Oh, my, how awful!" cried Jimmieboy.

"But it served him right. Don't you think so?" said the Dictionary.

"Yes, I do," said Jimmieboy. "But tell me. What'll I tell papa that he doesn't know?"

"Tell him that a sasspipedon is a barrel with four sides, and is open at both ends, and is a much better place for cigar ashes than his lap, because they pass through it to the floor, and so do not soil his clothes."

"Good!" said Jimmieboy, peering across the room to where his father still sat smoking. "I think I'll tell him now. Say, papa," he cried, sitting up, "what is a sasspipedon"

"I don't know. What?" answered Jimmieboy's father, laying his paper down, and coming over to where the little boy sat.

"It's a—it's a—it's an ash-barrel," said the

little fellow, trying to remember what the Dictionary had said.

"Who said so?" asked papa.

"The Dictionary," answered Jimmieboy.

And when Jimmieboy's father came to examine the Dictionary on the subject, the disagreeable old book hadn't a thing to say about the sasspipedon, and Jimmieboy went up to bed wondering what on earth it all meant, anyhow.

VI.

JIMMIEBOY'S SNOWMAN.

THE snow had been falling fast for well-nigh forty-eight hours and Jimmieboy was al-most crazy with delight. He loved the snow be-cause it was possible to do so much with it. One didn't need to go into a store, for instance, and part with ten cents every time one hap-pened to want a ball, when there was snow on the ground. Then, too, Jimmieboy had a new sled he wanted to try, but best of all, his father had promised to make him a snowman, with shoe-buttons for eyes and a battered old hat on his head, if perchance there could be found any-where in the house a hat of that sort. Fortu-nately a battered old hat was found, and the snowman when finished looked very well in it. I say fortunately because Jimmieboy had fully

made up his mind that a battered hat was absolutely necessary to make the snowman a success, and had not the old one been found I very
much fear the youth would have taken his
father's new one and battered that into the state
of usefulness required to complete the icy statue
to his satisfaction.

After the snowman was finished Jimmieboy
romped about him and shouted in great glee for
an hour or more, and then, growing a little
weary of the sport, he ran up into his nursery to
rest for a little while. He had not been there
very long however when he became, for some
unknown reason, uneasy about the funny looking creature he had left ehind him. Running to
the window he looked out to see if the snowman
was all right, and he was much surprised to
discover that he wasn't there at all. He couldn't
have melted, that was certain. for the air was
colder than it had been when the snowman was
put up. No one could have stolen him because
he was too big, and so, well, it certainly was a
strange conclusion, but none the less the only
one, he must have walked off himself.

"It's mighty queer!" thought Jimmieboy. "He
was there ten minutes ago."

Then he ran down stairs and peered out of the

window. At the front of the house no snowman
was in sight. Then he went to a side window
and looked out. Still no snowman. And then
the door-bell rang, and Jimmieboy went to the
door and opened it, and, dear me! how he laughed
when he saw who it was that had rung the bell,
as would also have you, for, honestly, it was no
one else than the snowman himself.

"What do you want?" asked Jimmieboy. The
snowman made a low bow to Jimmieboy, and
replied:

> "I got so weary standing there,
> I thought I'd ask you for a chair;
> 'Tis rather cool of me, I know,
> But coolness in a man of snow
> Is quite the fashion in these days,
> And to be stylish always pays."

"Won't you come in?" asked Jimmieboy
politely.

The snowman stared at Jimmieboy with all
the power of the shoe-buttons. He was evidently
surprised. In a moment or two, however, he
recovered and said:

> "Indeed, I'll enter not that door,
> I've tried it once or twice before."

"What of that?" asked Jimmieboy. "Didn't
you like it?"

"Oh, yes ; I liked it well enough,
  Although it used me pretty rough ;
  I lost a nose and foot and ear,
  Last time I happened to come here."

"Do you always speak in rhyme?" asked Jimmieboy, noticing the snowman's habit for the first time.

"Always, except when I speak in prose," said the snowman. "But perhaps you don't like rhyme?"

"Yes, I do like rhyme very much," said Jimmieboy.

"Then you like me," said the snowman, "because I'm mostly rime myself. But say, don't stand there with the door open letting all the heat out into the world. If you want to talk to me come outside where we can be comfortable."

"Very well," said Jimmieboy. "I'll come, if you'll wait until I bundle up a little so as to keep warm."

"All right, I'll wait," the snowman answered, "only don't you get too warm. I'll take you up to where I live and introduce you to my boys if you like—only hurry. If a thaw should set in we might have trouble.

"Of all mean things I ever saw
  The meanest of them is a thaw."

Jimmieboy, pondering deeply over his curious experience, quickly donned his overcoat and rubber boots, and in less time than it takes to tell it was out of doors again with the snowman. The huge white creature smiled happily as Jimmieboy came out, and taking him by the hand they went off up the road together.

"I'm glad you weren't offended with me because I wouldn't go in and sit down in your house," said the snowman, after they had walked a little way. "I had a very narrow escape thirty winters ago when I was young and didn't know any better than to accept an invitation of that sort. I lived in Russia then, and a small boy very much like you asked me to go into his house with him and see some funny picture-books he had. I said all right, and in I went, never thinking that the house was hot and that I'd be in danger of melting away. The boy got out his picture-books and we sat down before a blazing log fire. Suddenly the boy turned white as I was, and cried out:

"'Hi! What have you done with your leg?'

"'I brought it in with me, didn't I?' I said, looking down to where the leg ought to be, and noticing much to my concern that it was gone.

"'I thought so,' said the boy. 'Maybe you

left it down on the hat-rack with your hat and cane.'

"'Well I wish you'd go and see,' said I, very nervously. 'I don't want to lose that leg if I can help it.'

"So off the boy went," continued the snowman, "and I waited there before the fire wondering what on earth had become of the missing limb. The boy soon came back and announced that he couldn't find it.

"'Then I must hop around until I do find it,' I put in, starting up. "Would you believe it, Jimmieboy, that the minute I tried to rise and hop off on the search I discovered that my other leg was gone too?"

"Dear me!" said Jimmieboy. "How dreadful."

"It was fearful," returned the snowman, "but that wasn't half. I raised my hand to my forehead so as to think better, when off dropped my right arm, and as I reached out with my left to pick it up again that dropped off too. Then as my vest also disappeared, the boy cried out:

"'Why, I know what's the matter. You are melting away!'

"He was right. The heat of the log fire was just withering me right up. Fortunately as my neck began to go and my head rolled off the

chair onto the floor, the boy had presence of
mind enough to pick it up—it was all that was
left of me—and throw it out of the window. If
it hadn't been been for that timely act of his I
should have met the horrid fate of my cousin
the iceberg."

"What was that?" asked Jimmieboy.

"Oh, he wanted to travel," said the snowman,
"so he floated off down to South America and
waked up one morning to find himself nothing
but a tankful of the Gulf of Mexico. We never
saw the poor fellow again."

"I understand now why you didn't want to
come in," said Jimmieboy, "and I'm glad you
didn't do as I asked you, for I don't think mamma would have been pleased if you'd melted
away in the parlor."

"I know she wouldn't," said the snowman.
"She's like the woman mentioned in the poem,
who

> —— hated flies and muddy shoes,
> As well as pigs and kangaroos ;
> But most of all she did abhor,
> A melted snow-drift on the floor."

"Do you live near here?" asked Jimmieboy as
he trudged along at the snowman's side.

"Well," replied the snowman, "I do, and I

don't. When I do, I do, and when I don't, it's otherwise. This climate doesn't agree with me in the summer, and so when summer comes I move up to the North Pole. Ever been there?"

"No," said Jimmieboy, "what sort of a place is it?"

"Fine," returned the snowman. "The thermometer is always at least twenty miles below zero, even on the hottest days, and fire can't by any possibility come near us. Only one fire ever tried to and it was frozen stiff before it got within a hundred leagues of us. In winter, however, I come to places like this, and bring my little boys with me. We hire a convenient snowdrift and live in that. There's mine now right ahead of you."

Jimmieboy peered curiously along the road, at the far end of which he could see a huge mound of snow like the one the famous blizzard had piled up in front of his father's house some time before Jimmieboy and the world came to know each other.

"Do you live in that?" he asked.

"Yes," said the snowman. "And I will say that it's one of the most conveniently arranged snow-drifts I ever lived in. The house part of it is always as cold as ice—it's cooled by a special kind of refrigerator I had put in, which consumes about half a ton of ice a week."

Jimmieboy laughed.

"It's a cold furnace, eh?" he said.

"Precisely," answered the snowman. "And besides that the house is deliciously draughty so that we have no difficulty in keeping cold. Once in a while my boys run in the sun and get warmed through, but I dose 'em up with ice-water and cold cream and they soon get chilled again. But come, shall we go in?"

The pedestrians had by this time reached the side of the snow-drift, and Jimmieboy was pleased to see a door at one side of it. This the snowman opened, and they entered together a marvelously beautiful and extensive garden glistening with frosty flowers and snow-clad trees. At the end of the garden was a little white house that looked like the icing on Jimmieboy's birthday cake. As they approached it, the door of the little house was thrown open and a dozen small-sized snow boys rushed out and began to pelt the snowman and Jimmieboy with tennis balls.

"Hold up, boys," cried the snowman. "I've brought a friend home to see you."

The boys stopped at once, and Jimmieboy was

introduced to them. For hours they entertained him in the gardens and in the house. They showed him wondrous snow toys, among which were rocking horses, railway trains, soldiers —all made of the same soft fleecy substance from which the snowman and his children were constructed. When he had played for a long time with these they gave him caramels and taffy and cream cakes, these also made of snow, though as far as their taste went they were better than those made of sugar and chocolate and cream, or, at least, it seemed so to Jimmieboy at the time.

After this bit of luncheon the boys invited him out to coast, and he went along with them to the top of a high hill without any snow upon it, and for hours he and they slid from summit to base in great red-wheeled wagons. It took his breath away the first time he went down, but when he got used to it he found the sport delightful. He was glad, however, when a voice from the little white house called to the children to return.

"Come in now, boys," it said. "It is getting too warm for you to stay out."

The boys were obedient to the word and they all—a dozen of them at least—trooped back into

the house where Jimmieboy was welcomed by
his friend the snowman again. The snowman
looked a little anxious, Jimmieboy thought, but
he supposed this was because the littlest snow-
boy had overheated himself at his play and had
come in minus two fingers and an ear. It was
not this, however, that bothered him, as Jimmieboy found out in a few minutes, for the snowman simply restored the missing fingers and the
ear by making a new lot for the little fellow out
of a handful of snow he got in the garden. Anything so easily replaced was not worth worry-
ing over. The real cause of his anxiety came
out when the father of this happy little family
of snow boys called Jimmieboy to one side.

"You must go home right away," he said. "I'm
sorry, but we have got to fly just as hard as we
can or we are lost."

"But——" said Jimmieboy.

"Don't ask for reasons," returned the snowman, gathering his little snowboys together and
rushing off with them in tow. "I haven't time to
give them. Just read that and you'll see. Fare-
well."

Then he made off down the garden path, and
as he fled with his babies Jimmieboy picked up
the thing the snowman had told him to read,

and wandered back into the house, holding it in his hand. It was only a newspaper, but at the top of the first column was an announcement in huge letters:

WARM WAVE TO-NIGHT.

WISE SNOWMEN WILL MOVE NORTH AT ONCE.

When Jimmieboy saw this he knew right away why he had been deserted, but to this day he doesn't know how he knew it, because at the time this happened he had not learned how to read. At all events he discovered what the trouble was instantly, and then he decided that as he had been left by all of his new friends he would go home. He walked to the front door and opened it, and what do you suppose it opened into?

The garden?

Not a bit of it.

Into Jimmieboy's nursery itself, and when the door closed upon him after he had stepped through it into the nursery and Jimmieboy turned to look at it, lo, and behold it wasn't there!

Nor was the snowman to be found the next morning. It was quite evident that he had got away from the warm wave that appeared on the scene the night before, for there wasn't even a sign of the shoe-button eyes or the battered hat, as there certainly would have been had he melted instead of run away.

VII.

THE BICYCLOPÆDIA BIRD.

"BOO!" said something.

And Jimmieboy of course was startled. So startled was he that, according to his own statement, he jumped ninety-seven feet, though for my own part I don't believe he really jumped more than thirty-three. He was too sleepy to count straight anyhow. He had been lolling under his canvas tent down near the tennis-court all the afternoon, getting lazier and lazier every minute, and finally he had turned over square on his back, put his head on a small cushion his mamma had made for him, closed his eyes, and then came the "Boo!"

"I wonder—" he said, as he gazed about him, seeing no sign of any creature that could by any possibility say "Boo!" however.

"Of course you do. That's why I've come," interrupted a voice from the bushes. "More children of your age suffer from the wonders than from measles, mumps, or canthaves."

"What are canthaves?" asked Jimmieboy.

"Canthaves are things you can't have. Don't you ever suffer because you can't have things?" queried the voice.

"Oh, yes, indeed!" returned Jimmieboy. "Lots and lots of times."

"And didn't you ever have the wonders so badly that you got cross and wouldn't eat anything but sweet things for dinner?" the voice asked.

"I don't know exactly what you mean by the wonders," replied Jimmieboy.

"Why, wonders is a disease that attacks boys who want to know why things are and can't find out," said the voice.

"Oh, my, yes I've had that lots of times," laughed Jimmieboy. "Why, only this morning I asked my papa why there weren't any dandelionesses, and he wouldn't tell me because he said he had to catch a train, and I've been wondering why ever since."

"I thought you'd had it; all boys do get it sooner or later, and it's a thing you can have any number of times unless you have me around," said the voice.

"What are you anyhow?" asked Jimmieboy.

"I'm what they call the Bicyclopædia Bird. I'm a regular owl for wisdom. I know everything—just like the Cyclopædia; and I have two wheels instead of legs, which is why they call me the Bicyclopædia Bird. I can't let you see me, because these are not my office hours. I can only be seen between ten and two on the thirty-second of March every seventeenth year. You can get a fair idea of what I look like from my photograph, though."

As the voice said this, sure enough a photograph did actually pop out of the bush, and land at Jimmieboy's feet. He sprang forward eagerly, stooped, and picking it up, gazed earnestly at it. And a singular creature the Bicyclopædia Bird must have been if the photograph did him justice. He had the head of an owl, but his body was oblong in shape, just like a book, and, as the voice had said, in place of legs were two wheels precisely like those of a bicycle. The effect was rather pleasing, but so funny that Jimmieboy really wanted to laugh. He did not laugh, however, for fear of hurting the Bird's feelings, which the Bird noticed and appreciated.

"Thank you," he said, simply.

"What for?" asked Jimmieboy, looking up from the photograph, and peering into the bush

in the vain hope of catching a glimpse of the Bird itself.

"For not laughing," replied the Bird. "If you

had laughed I should have biked away at once because I am of no value to any one who laughs at my personal appearance. It always makes me forget all I know, and that does me up for a whole year. If I forget all I know, you see, I have to study hard to learn it all over again, and that's a tremendous job, considering how much knowledge there is to be had in the world. So you see, by being polite and kind enough not to laugh at me, who can't help being funny to look at, and who am not to blame for looking that way, because I am not a self-made Bird, you are really the gainer, for I promise you I'll tell you anything you want to know."

"That's very nice of you," returned Jimmieboy; "and perhaps, to begin with, you'll tell me something that I ought to want to know, whether I do or not."

"That is a very wise idea," said the Bicyclopædia Bird, "and I'll try to do it. Let me see; now, do you know why the Pollywog is always amiable?"

"No," returned Jimmieboy. "I never even knew that he was, and so couldn't really wonder why."

"But you wonder why now, don't you?" asked the voice, anxiously. "For if you don't, I can't tell you."

"I'm just crazy to know," Jimmieboy responded.

"Then listen, and I will tell you," said the voice. And then the strange bird recited this poem about

THE POLLYWOG.

"The Pollywog's a perfect type
    Of amiability.
He never uses angry speech
    Wherever he may be.
He never calls his brother names,
    Or tweaks his sister's nose;
He never pulls the sea-dog's tail,
    Or treads upon his toes.

"He never says an unkind word,
    And frown he never will.
A smile is ever on his lips,
    E'en when he's feeling ill.
And this is why: when Pollywog
    The first came on the scene,
He had a temper like a cat's—
    His eye with it was green.

"Now, just about the time when he
    Began to lose his tail,
To change into a croaking frog,
    He came across a nail—
A nail so rusty that it looked
    Just like an angle-worm,
Except that it was straight and stiff,
    And so could never squirm.

"And Polly, feeling hungry, to
    Assuage his appetite,
Swam boldly up to that old nail,
    And gave it such a bite,
He nearly broke his upper jaw ;
    His lower jaw he bent.
And then he got so very mad,
    His temper simply went.

"He lost it so completely as
    He lashed and gnashed around,
That though this happened years ago,
    It has not since been found.
And that is why, at all times, in
    The Pollywog you see,
A model of that virtue rare—
    True Amiability."

"Now, I dare say," continued the Bird—"I dare
say you might have asked your father—who
really knows a great deal, considering he isn't
my twin brother—sixteen million four hundred
and twenty-three times why the Pollywog is always so good-natured, and he couldn't have answered you more than once out of the whole lot,
and he'd have been wrong even then."

"It must be lovely to know so much," said
Jimmieboy.

"It is," said the Bird; "that is, it is lovely
when you don't have to keep it all to yourself.
It's very nice to tell things. That's really the

best part of secrets, I think. It is such fun telling them. Now, why does the sun rise in the
morning"

"I don't know. Why?"

"For the same reason that you do," returned
the sage Bird. "Because it is time to get up."

"Well, here's a thing I don't know about,"
said Jimmieboy. "What is 'to alarm?'"

"To frighten—to scare—to discombobulate,"
replied the Bird. "Why?"

"Well, I don't see why an alarm-clock is called
an alarm-clock, because it doesn't ever alarm
anybody," said Jimmieboy.

"Oh, it doesn't, eh?" cried the Bird. "Well,
that's just where you are mistaken. It alarms
the people or the animals you dream about when
you are asleep, and they make such a noise getting away that they wake you up. Why, an
alarm-clock saved my life once. I dreamed that
I fell asleep on board a steamboat that went so
fast hardly anybody could stay on board of her
—she just regularly slipped out from under their
feet, and unless a passenger could run fast
enough to keep up with her, or was chained fast
enough to keep aboard of her, he'd get dropped
astern every single time. I dreamed I was aboard
of her one day, and that to keep on deck I

chained myself to the smoke-stack, and then
dozed off. Just as I was dozing, a Misinforma-
tion Bird, who was jealous of me, sneaked up
and cut the chain. As he expected, the minute
I was cut loose the boat rushed from under me,
and the first thing I knew I was struggling in the
water. While I was struggling there, I was attacked by a Catfish. Cats are death to birds,
you know, and I really had given myself up for
lost, when '*ting-a-ling-a-ling-a-ling*' went the
alarm-clock in the corner of my cage; the fish
turned blue with fear, swished his tail about in
his fright, and the splashing of the water waked
me up, and there I was standing on one wheel on
my perch, safe and sound. If that clock hadn't
gone off and alarmed that Catfish, I am afraid
I should have been forever lost to the world."

"I see now; but I never knew before why it was
called an alarm-clock, and I've wondered about
it a good deal," said Jimmieboy. "Now, here's
another thing I've bothered over many a time:
What's the use of weeds?"

"Oh, that's easy," said the Bird, with a laugh.
"To make lawns look prettier next year than
they do this."

"I don't see how that is," said Jimmieboy.

"Clear as window-glass. This year you have
weeds on your lawn, don't you?"

" Yes," returned Jimmieboy.

" And you make them get out, don't you?" said the Bird.

" Yes," assented Jimmieboy.

" Well, there you are. By getting out they make your lawns prettier. That's one of the simplest things in the world. But here's a thing I should think you'd wonder at. Why do houses have shutters on their windows?" asked the Bird.

" I know why," said Jimmieboy. " It's to keep the sun out."

" That's nonsense, because the sun is so much larger than any house that was ever built it couldn't get in if it tried," returned the feathered sage.

" Then I don't know why. Why?" asked Jimmieboy.

" So as to wake people up by banging about on windy nights, and they are a mighty useful invention too," said the Bird. " I knew of a whole family that got blown away once just because they hadn't any shutters to bang about and warn them of their danger. It was out in the West, where they have cyclones, which are things that pick up houses and toss them about just as you would pebbles. A Mr. and Mrs. Podlington had built a house in the middle of a big field for

themselves and their seventeen children. Mr.
Podlington was very rich, but awful mean, and
when the house was finished, all except the shutters, he said he wasn't going to have any shutters because they cost too much, and so they
hadn't a shutter on the house. One night after
they had lived where they were about six months
they all went to bed about nine o'clock, and by
ten they were sound asleep, every one of them.
At eleven o'clock a breeze sprang up. This
grew very shortly into a gale. Then it became a hurricane, and by two o'clock it was a
cyclone. One cyclone wouldn't have hurt much,
but at three o'clock two more came along, and
the first thing the Podlington family knew their
house was blown off its foundations, lifted high
up in the air, and at breakfast-time was out of
sight, and, what is worse, it has never come
down anywhere, and all this happened ten years
ago."

"But where did it go?" asked Jimmieboy.

"Nobody knows. Maybe it landed in the moon.
Maybe it's being blown about on the wings of
those cyclones yet. I don't believe we'll ever
know," answered the Bird. "But you can see
just why that all happened. It was Mr. Podlington's meanness about the shutters, and nothing

else. If he had had shutters on that house, at least one of them would have flopped bangety-bang against the house all night, and the chances are that they would all have been waked up by it before the cyclone came, and in plenty of time to save themselves. In fact, I think very likely they could have fastened the house more securely to the ground, and saved it too, if they had waked up and seen what was going on."

"I'll never build a house without shutters," said Jimmieboy, as he tried to fancy the condition of the Podlingtons whisking about in the air for ten long years—nearly five years longer than he himself had lived. If they had landed in the moon it wouldn't have been so bad, but this other possible and even more likely fate of mounting on the wind ever higher and higher and not landing anywhere was simply dreadful to think about.

"I wouldn't, especially in the cyclone country," returned the voice in the bush. "But I'll tell you of one thing that would save you if you really did have to build a house without shutters; build it with wings. You've heard of houses with wings, of course?"

"Yes, indeed," said Jimmieboy. "Why, our house has three wings. One of 'em was put on it

"I'LL NEVER BUILD A HOUSE WITHOUT SHUTTERS."

last summer, so that we could have a bigger kitchen."

"I remember," said the Bird. "I wondered a good deal about that wing until I found out it was for a kitchen, and not to fly with. The house had enough wings to fly with without the new one. In fact, the new one for flying purposes would be as useless as a third wheel to a bicycle."

"What do you mean by to fly with?" asked Jimmieboy, puzzled at this absurd remark of the Bird.

"Exactly what I say. Wings are meant to fly with, aren't they? I hope you knew that!" said the Bird. "So if the Podlingtons' house had had wings it might have got back all right. It could have worked its way slowly out of the cyclone, and then sort of rested on its wings a little until it was prepared to swoop down on to its old foundations, alighting just where it was before. A trip through the air under such circumstances would have been rather pleasant, I think —much pleasanter than going off into the air forever, without any means of getting back."

"But," asked Jimmieboy, "even if Mr. Podlington's house had had wings, how could he have made them work?"

"Why, how stupid of you!" cried the Bird. "Don't you know that he could have taken hold of the——"

"Ting-a-ling-a-ling a-ling-a-ling!" rang the alarm-clock up in the cook's room, which had been set for six o'clock in the afternoon instead of for six in the morning by some odd mistake of Mary Ann's.

"The alarm! The alarm!" shrieked the Bird, in terror.

And then the invisible creature, if Jimmieboy could judge by the noise in the bush, seemed to make off as fast as he could go, his cries of fear growing fainter and fainter as the wise Bird got farther and farther away, until finally they died away in the distance altogether.

Jimmieboy sprang to his feet, looked down the road along which his strange friend had fled, and then walked into the house, wishing that the alarm-clock had held off just a little longer, so that he might have learned how the wings of a house should be managed to make the house fly off into the air. He really felt as if he would like to try the experiment with his own house.

VIII.

GIANT THE JACK KILLER.

JIMMIEBOY was turning over the pages of his fairy book the other night, trying to refresh his memory concerning the marvelous doings of the fairy-land people by looking at the pictures. His papa was too tired to read to him, and as no one else in the house was willing to undertake the task, the boy was doing his best to entertain himself, and as it happened he got more out of his own efforts than he ever derived from the efforts of others. He had dallied long over the weird experiences of Cinderella, and had just turned over the pages which lead up to the story of Jack the Giant Killer, when something in the picture of the Giant's castle seemed to move.

Looking a little more closely at the picture in

a startled sort of way, Jimmieboy saw that the moving thing was the knob of the castle door, and in a jiffy the door itself opened, and a huge homely creature whom Jimmieboy recognized at once as an ogre stuck his head out. For a moment the little fellow felt disposed to cry for help. Surely if the Giant could open the door in the picture there was no reason why he should not step out of the book entirely and make a speedy meal of Jimmieboy, who, realizing that he was entirely unarmed, was inclined to run and hide behind his papa's back. His fast oozing courage was quickly restored, however, by the Giant himself, who winked at him in a genial sort of fashion as much as to say: "Nonsense, boy, I wouldn't eat you, if I could." The wink he followed up at once with a smile, and then he said:

"That you, Jimmieboy?"

"Yes, sir," said Jimmieboy, very civilly indeed. "I'm me. Are you you?"

The Giant laughed.

"Yes," he replied, "and so, of course, we are ourselves. Are you very busy?"

"Not very," said Jimmieboy. "Why?"

"I want a little advice from you," the Giant answered. "I think it's about time the tables were turned on that miserable little ruffian Jack.

The idea of a big thing like me being killed every day of his life by a mosquito like Jack is very tiresome, and I want to know if you don't think it would be fair if I should kill him just once for the sake of variety. It won't hurt him. He'll come to life again right away just as we Giants do——"

"Don't you stay dead when Jack kills you?" asked Jimmieboy.

"You know the answer to that as well as I do," said the Giant. "You've had this story read to you every day now for three years, haven't you?"

"About that," said Jimmieboy.

"Well, if we staid dead how do you suppose we'd be on hand to be killed again the next time you had the story read to you?"

"I never thought of that," said Jimmieboy.

"Never thought of it?" echoed the ogre. "Why, what kind of thoughts do you think, anyhow? It's the only thought for a thinker to think I think, don't you think so?"

"Say that again, will you?" said Jimmieboy.

"Couldn't possibly," said the ogre. "In fact, I've forgotten it. But what do you think of my scheme? Don't you think it would be wise if I killed Jack just once?"

"Perhaps it would," said the boy. "That is if it wouldn't hurt him."

"Hurt him? Didn't I tell you it wouldn't hurt him?" said the Giant. "I wouldn't hurt that boy for all the world. If I did I'd lose my position. Why, all I am I owe to him. The fairy people let me live in this magnificent castle for nothing. They let me rob them of all their property, and all I have to do in return for this is to be killed by Jack whenever any little boy or girl in your world desires to be amused by a tragedy of that sort. So you see I haven't any hard feelings against him, even if I did call him a miserable little ruffian."

"Well, I don't exactly like to have Jack killed," said Jimmieboy. "I've always rather liked him. What do you suppose he would say to it?"

"That's just the point. I wouldn't kill him unless he was willing. That would be a violation of my agreement with him, and when he came to he might sue me for what the lawyers call a breach of contract." said the ogre. "Now, it seemed to me that if you were to go to Jack and tell him that you were getting a little tired of having this story end the way it does all the time, and that you thought it only fair to me that I should have a chance to celebrate a victory, say once a week—every Saturday night for instance—he'd be willing to do it."

"Where can I find him" asked Jimmieboy. "I just as lief ask him."

"He's in the picture, two pages farther along, sharpening his sword," said the ogre.

"Very well, I'll go see him at once," said Jimmieboy. Then he said good-by to the Giant, and turned over the pages until he came to the pictures showing how Jack sharpened his sword on the soles of the shoes of another giant, whom he had bound and strapped to the floor.

At first Jimmieboy did not know how to address him. He had often spoken to the figures in the pictures, but they had never replied to anything he had said. However, he made a beginning.

"Ahem!" he said.

The effect was pleasing, for as he said this Jack stopped sharpening his blade and turned to see who had spoken.

"Ah, Jimmieboy!" said the small warrior. "Howdy do. Haven't seen much of you this week. You've been paying more attention to Hop o' My Thumb than to me lately."

"Well, I love you just the same," said Jimmieboy. "I've just seen the Giant that lives up in the castle with the dragon on the front stoop."

"He's a good fellow," said Jack. "I'm very fond of him. He never gives me any trouble, and dies just as easy as if he were falling off a log, and out of business hours we're great chums. He's had something on his mind lately, though, that I don't understand. He says being killed every day is getting monotonous."

"That's what he said to me," said Jimmieboy.

"Well, I hope he doesn't resign his position," said Jack, thoughtfully. "I know it isn't in every way a pleasant one, but he might go farther and fare worse. The way I kill him is painless, but if he got into that Bean-staĩk boy's hands he'd be all bruised up. You can't fall a mile without getting hurt, you know, and I like the old fellow too well to have him go over to that Bean-stalk cousin of mine."

"He likes you, too," said Jimmieboy, pleased to find that there was so much good feeling between the two creatures. "But he thinks he ought to get a chance to win once in a while. He said if he could arrange it with you to have him kill you once a week—Saturday nights, for instance —he'd be perfectly contented.

"That's reasonable enough," said Jack, nodding his head approvingly. "Did he say how he would like to do it?"

"No, only that he'd kill you tenderly, so that you wouldn't suffer," said Jimmieboy.

"Oh, I know that!" said Jack, softly. "He's too tender-hearted to hurt anybody. I'm very much inclined to agree to the proposition, but he must let me choose the manner of the killing. He hasn't had much practice killing people, and if he were to do it by hitting me on the head with a stick of wood I'd be likely to wake up with a headache next day; neither should I like to be smothered because while that doesn't bruise one or break any bones its awfully stuffy, and if there's one thing I like it is fresh air."

"Perhaps he might eat you," suggested Jimmieboy.

"He isn't big enough to do that comfortably," said Jack, shaking his head. "He'd have to cut me up and chew me, because his throat isn't large enough for him to swallow me at one gulp. But I'll tell you what you can do. You go back to him, and tell him that I'll agree to his proposition, if he'll have me cooked in a plum-pudding four hundred feet in circumference. I'm very fond of plum-pudding, and while he is eating it from the outside I could be eating it from the inside, and, of course, I shouldn't be burned in the cooking, because in the middle of a pudding of that size the heat never could reach me."

"But when he reached you," said Jimmieboy, "you'd have the same trouble you said you'd have if he ate you up. He'd have to cut you to pieces and chew you."

"Ah!" said Jack, "don't you see my point? By the time he reached me he would have eaten so much plum-pudding that he wouldn't have room for me, so I'd escape."

"But, then, you wouldn't be killed," said Jimmieboy.

"That wouldn't make any difference," said Jack. "We'd stop the story before I escaped and everybody would think I'd been eaten up, and that's all he wants. He just wants to seem to win once. He doesn't really care about killing me dead. Don't you see."

"Yes, I think I do," said Jimmieboy, "and I'll go back and tell him what you say."

"Thank you," said Jack. "And while you are there give him my love, and tell him I'll be around to kill him as usual after tea."

All of which Jimmieboy did and the Giant readily agreeing to the plum-pudding scheme, said good-night to his little visitor, and retired into the castle, closing the door after him.

Then Jimmieboy went to bed in a great hurry, because he knew how sleep made time seem shorter than it really was, and he was very anxious to have Saturday night come around so that he could see how the new ending to the story of Jack the Giant Killer worked.

As yet that Saturday night has not turned up, so that I really cannot tell you whether or not the arrangement was a success.

IX.

JIMMIEBOY AND THE FIREWORKS.

THERE was whispering going on somewhere, and Jimmieboy felt that it was his duty to find out where it was, who it was that was doing it, and what it was that was being whispered. It was about an hour after supper on the evening of July 3d when it all happened. A huge box full of fireworks had arrived only a few hours before, and Jimmieboy was somewhat afraid that the whisperings might have come from burglars who, knowing that there were thirty-five rockets, twenty Roman candles, colored lights by the dozen, and no end of torpedoes and fire-crackers and other things in the house, had come to steal them, and, if he could help himself, Jimmieboy was not going to allow that. So he began to search about, and in a few minutes he had located the whisperers in the very room at the foot of the back stairs in which the fireworks were. His little heart almost stopped beating for a moment when he realized this. It isn't pleasant to feel that perhaps you will be deprived, after all, of something you have looked forward to for a whole month, and upon the very eve of the fulfillment of your dearest hopes at that.

"I'll have to tell papa about this," he said; and then, realizing that his papa was not at home, and that his mamma was up stairs trying to convince his small brother that it would be impossible to get the moon into the nursery, although it looked much smaller even than the nursery window, Jimmieboy resolved that he would take the matter in hand himself.

"A boygler wouldn't hurt me, and maybe if I talk gruff and keep out of sight, he'll think I'm papa and run," he said.

Then he tried his gruff voice, and it really was tremendously gruff—about as gruff as the bark of a fox-terrier. After he had done this, he tiptoed softly down the stairs until he stood directly opposite the door of the room where the fireworks were.

"Move on, you boygler you!" he cried, just as he thought his father would have said it.

The answer was an explosion—not exactly of fireworks, but of mirth.

"He thinks somebody's trying to steal us," said a funny little voice, the like of which Jimmieboy had never heard before.

"How siss-siss-sissingular of him," said another voice that sounded like a fire-cracker missing fire.

THE GIANT CRACKER SINGING HIS SONG.

"He thinks he can fool us by imitating the voice of his pop-pop-pop-popper," put in a third voice, with a laugh.

At which Jimmieboy opened the door and looked in, and then he saw whence the whispering had come, and to say that he was surprised at what he saw is a too mild way of putting it.

He was so astonished that he lost all control over his joints, and the first thing he knew he was sitting on the floor. The spectacle had, in fact, knocked him over, as well it might, for there, walking up and down the floor, swarming over chairs and tables, playing pranks with each other, and acting in a generally strange fashion, were the fire-works themselves. It was interesting, and at the same time alarming, for one or two reckless sky-rockets were smoking, a lot of foolish little fire-crackers were playing with matches in one corner, and a number of the great big cannon torpedoes were balancing themselves on the arms of the gas-fixture, utterly heedless of the fact that if they were to fall to the floor they would explode and be done for forever.

"Hullo, Jimmieboy!" said one of the larger rockets, taking off his funny little cap at the astonished youngster. "I suppose you've come down to see us rehearse?"

"I thought somebody was stealing you, and I came down to frighten them away," Jimmieboy replied.

The Rocket laughed. "Nobody can steal us," it said. "If anybody came to steal us, we'd cry, and get so soaked with tears nobody could get us to go off, so what good would we be?"

"Not much, I guess," said Jimmieboy.

"That's the answer," returned the Rocket. "You seem to be good at riddles. Let me give you another. What's the difference between a man who steals a whole wig and a fire-cracker?"

"I am sure I don't know," said Jimmieboy, still too full of wonderment to think out an answer to a riddle like that.

"Why, one goes off with a whole head of hair," said the Rocket, "and the other goes off only with a bang."

"That's good," said Jimmieboy. "Make it up yourself?"

"No," said the Rocket. "I got that out of the magazine."

"What magazine?" asked Jimmieboy, innocently.

"The powder-magazine," roared the Rocket, and then the Pin Wheel and other fire-works danced about, and threw themselves on the floor with laughter—all except the Torpedoes, which jumped up and down on a soft plush chair, where they were safe.

When the laughter over the Rocket's wit had subsided, one of the Roman Candles called to the Giant Cracker, and asked him to sing a song for Jimmieboy.

"I can't sing to-night," said the Cracker.
"I'm very busy making ready my report for to-morrow."

Here the Cracker winked at Jimmieboy, as much as to say, "How is that for a joke?" Whereat Jimmieboy winked back to show that he thought it wasn't bad; which so pleased the Cracker that he said he guessed, after all, he would sing his song if the little Crackers would stop playing until he got through. The little Crackers promised, and the Giant Cracker sang this song:

"THE GIANT CRACKER AND THE MANDARIN'S
DAUGHTER.

" He was a Giant Cracker bold,
    His name was Wing-Hi-Ee.
He wore a dress of red and gold—
    Was handsome as could be.
His master was a Mandarin,
    Who lived in old Shang-Hai,
And had a daughter named Ah Din,
    With sweet blue almond eye.

"Now Wing he loved this Saffron Queen,
    And Ah Din she loved him ;
But Chinese law came in between
    Them with its measures grim.
For you must know, in that far land,
    Where dwell the heathen wild,
A Cracker may not win the hand
    Of any noble's child.

"This made their love a hopeless one—
 Alas! that it should be
That anywhere beneath the sun
 Exists such misery!
So they resolved, since she could not
 Become his cherished bride,
Together they'd seek out some spot
 And there they'd suicide.

"They hastened, weeping, from the town,
 Wing-Hi and fair Ah Din,
And on the river-bank sat down
 Until the tide came in.
Then Wing-Hi whispered, sitting there,
 With tear-drops in his eye,
'Good-by, Ah Din!' And, in despair,
 She answered him, 'Good-by.'

"And then she grasped a sulphur match;
 She lit it on her shoe,
Whereat, with neatness and dispatch,
 Wing-Hi she touched it to.
There came a flash, there came a shriek,
 A sound surpassing weird,
And Wing-Hi brave and Ah Din meek
 In pieces disappeared."

"Isn't that lovely?" asked the Rocket, his
voice husky with emotion.

"It's very fine," said Jimmieboy. "It's rather
sad, though."

"Yes; but it might have been sadder, you
know," said the Giant Cracker. "She might not

have loved him at all; and if she hadn't loved him, he wouldn't have wasted a match committing suicide for her sake, and then there wouldn't have been any tragedy, and, of course, no song would have been written about it. Why, there is no end to the misery there might have been."

Here one of the Torpedoes fell off the gas-fixture to the floor, where he exploded with a loud noise. There was a rush from all sides to see whether the poor little fellow was done for forever.

"Send for the doctor," said the Pin Wheel. "I think he can be mended."

"No, don't," said the injured Torpedo. "I can fix myself up again. Send for a whisk broom and bring me a parlor match, and I'll be all right."

"What's the whisk broom for?" asked Jimmieboy, somewhat surprised at the remedies suggested.

"Why," said the Torpedo, "if you will sweep me together with the whisk broom and wrap me up carefully, I'll eat the head off the parlor match, and I'll be all right again. The match head will give me all the snap I need, and if you'll wrap me up in the proper way, I'll show you what noise is to-morrow. You'll think I'm some relation to that Miss Din in the Giant Cracker's song, unless I'm mistaken, when you hear me explode.

The Fire-crackers jeered a little at this, because there has always been more or less jealousy between the Torpedoes and the Fire-crackers, but the Rocket soon put a stop to their sneers.

"What's the use of jeering?" he said. "You don't know whether he'll make much noise or not. The chances are he'll make more noise than a great many of you Crackers, who are just as likely as not to turn out sissers in the long-run."

The Fire-crackers were very much abashed by the Rocket's rebuke, and retired shamefacedly into their various packs, whereupon the Pin Wheel suggested that the Rocket recite his poem telling the singular story of Nate and the Rocket.

"Would you like to hear that story, Jimmieboy?" asked the Rocket.

"Very much," said Jimmieboy. "The name of it sounds interesting."

"Well, I'll try to tell it. It's pretty long, and your ears are short; but we can try it, as the boy observed to the man who said he didn't think the boy's mouth was large enough to hold four pieces of strawberry short-cake. So here goes. The real title of the poem is

"THE DREADFUL FATE OF NAUGHTY NATE.

"'Way back in eighty-two or three—
    I don't recall the date—
There lived somewhere—'twixt you and me,
    I really can't locate
The place exact; say Sangaree—
    A lad; we'll call him Nate.

"His father was a grocer, or
    A banker, or maybe
He kept a thriving candy store,
    For all that's known to me.
Perhaps he was the Governor
    Of Maine or Floridee.

"At any rate, he had a dad—
    Or so the story's told;
Most youngsters that I've known have had—
    And Nate's had stacks of gold,
And those who knew him used to add,
    He spent it free and bold.

"If Nate should ask his father for
    A dollar or a cent,
His father'd always give him more
    Than for to get he went;
And then, before the day was o'er,
    Nate always had it spent.

"Molasses taffy, circus, cake,
    Tarts, soda-water, pie,
Hot butter-scotch, or rare beefsteak,
    Or silk hats, Nate could buy.
His father'd never at him shake
    His head and ask him 'Why?'

"'For but one thing,' his father cried,
   'You must not spend your store;
Sky-rockets I cannot abide,
   So buy them never more.
Let such, I pray, be never spied
   Inside of my front door.'

"But Nate, alas! did not obey
   His father's orders wise.
He hied him forth without delay,
   Ignoring tarts and pies,
And bought a rocket huge, size A,
   'The Monarch of the Skies.'

"He clasped it tightly to his breast,
   And smiled a smile of glee;
And as the sun sank in the west,
   He sat beneath a tree,
And then the rocket he invest-
   I-g-a-t-e-d.

"Alas for Nate! The night was warm;
   June-bugs and great fire-flies
Around about his head did swarm;
   The mercury did rise;
And then a fine electric storm
   Played havoc in the skies.

"Now if, perchance, it was a fly,
   I'm not prepared to say;
Or if 'twas lightning from the sky,
   That came along that way;
Or if 'twas only brought on by
   The heat of that warm day,

"I am not certain, but 'tis clear
   There came a sudden boom,
And high up in the atmosphere,
   Enlightening the gloom,
The rocket flew, a fiery spear,
   And Nate, too, I presume.

NATE AS A COMET.

"For never since that July day
   Has any man seen Nate.
But far off in the Milky Way,
   Astronomers do state,
A comet brilliant, so they say,
   Doth round about gyrate.

"It's head's so like small Natty's face,
  They think it's surely he,
Aboard that rocket-stick in space,
  Still mounting constantly ;
And still must mount until no trace
  Of it at all we see."

"Isn't that the most fearfully awfully terribly horribly horribly terribly fearful bit of awfulness you ever heard?" queried the Rocket, when he had finished.

"It is indeed," said Jimmieboy. "It really makes me feel unhappy, and I wish you hadn't told it to me."

"I would not bother about it," said the Rocket; "because really the best thing about it is that it never happened."

"Suppose it did happen," said Jimmieboy, after thinking it over for a minute or two. "Would Nate ever get back home again?"

"Oh, he might," returned the Rocket. "But not before six or seven million years, and that would make him late for tea, you know. By-the-way," the Rocket added, "do you know the best kind of tea to have on Fourth of July?"

"No," said Jimmieboy. "What?"

"R-o-c-k-e-tea," said the Rocket.

The Pin Wheels laughed so heartily at this

that one of them fell over on a box of Blue Lights
and set them off, and the Rocket endeavoring to
put them out was set going himself, and the
first thing Jimmieboy knew, his friend gave a
fearful siss, and disappeared up the chimney.
The sparks from the Rocket falling on the Roman
Candles started them along, and three or four
balls from them landed on a flower piece which
was soon putting forth the most beautiful fiery
roses imaginable, one of which, as it gave its dy-
ing sputter, flew up and landed on the fuse of a
great set piece that was supposed to have a motto
on it.   Jimmieboy was almost too frightened to
move, so he just sat where he was, and stared
at the set piece until he could read the motto,
which was, strange to say, no motto at all, but
simply these words in red, white, and blue fire,
"Wake up, and go to bed right."   Whereupon
Jimmieboy rubbed his eyes, and opened them
wider than ever to find his papa bending over
him, and saying the very words he had seen on
the set piece.

Probably the reason why his papa was saying
this was that Jimmieboy had been found by him
on his return home lying fast asleep, snuggled
up in the corner of the library lounge.

As for the fire-works, in some way or other

they all managed to get back into the box again in good condition, except the broken torpedo, which was found in the middle of the floor just where it had fallen. Which Jimmieboy thinks was very singular.

X.

JIMMIEBOY'S PHOTOGRAPH.

JIMMIEBOY had been taken to the photographer's and had posed several times for the man who made pictures of little boys. One picture showed how he looked leaning against a picket fence with a tiger skin rug under his feet. Another showed him in the act of putting his hands into his pockets, while a third was a miserable attempt to show how he looked when he couldn't stand still. The last pleased Jimmieboy very much. It made him laugh and Jimmieboy liked laughing better than anything, perhaps, excepting custard, which was his idea of real solid bliss. Why it made him laugh, I do not know, unless it was because in the picture he was very much blurred and looked something like a mixture of a cloud and a pin-wheel.

"I like that one," Jimmieboy said to his mother, when the proof came home. "Won't you let me have it?"

"Yes," said his mother. "You can have it. I don't think any one else wants it."

So the proof became Jimmieboy's property, and he put it away in his collection of treasures, which already contained many valuable things, such as the whistle of a rubber ball, a piece of elastic, and a worn-out tennis racket. These treasures the boy used to have out two or three times a day, and the last time he had them out something queer happened. The blurred little figure in the picture spoke to him and told him something he didn't forget in a hurry.

"You think I'm a funny-looking thing don't you?" said the blurred picture of himself.

"Yes, I do," said Jimmieboy, "that's why I laugh at you whenever I see you."

"Well, I laugh when I see you, too," retorted the picture. "You are just as funny to look at sometimes as I am."

"I'm not either," said Jimmieboy. "I don't look like a cloud or a pin-wheel, and you do."

"I'm a picture of you, just the same," returned the proof, "and if you had stood still when the man was taking you, I'd have been all right. It's

awful mean the way little boys have of not standing still when they are having their pictures
taken, and then laughing at the thing they're
responsible for afterward."

"I didn't mean to be mean," said Jimmieboy.

"Perhaps not," retorted the picture, "but if it
hadn't been for you I'd have been a lovely picture, and your mamma would have had a nice
little silver frame put around me, and maybe
I'd have been standing on your papa's desk with
the inkstand and the mucilage instead of having
to live all my life with a broken whistle and a
tennis bat that nobody but you has any use for."

Here the picture sighed, and Jimmieboy felt
very sorry for it.

"Boys don't know what a terrible lot of horrid
things happen because they don't stand still
sometimes," continued the picture. "I know of
lots of cases where untold misery has come from
movey boys."

"From what?" queried Jimmieboy.

"Movey boys," replied the picture. "By that I
mean boys that don't stand still when they
ought to. Why, I knew of a boy once who
wouldn't stand still and he shook a whole town
to pieces."

"Ho!" jeered Jimmieboy. "I don't believe it."

"Well, it's so, whether you believe it or not." said the picture. "The boy's name was Bob, and he lived somewhere, I don't remember where. His mother told him to stand still and he wouldn't; he just jumped up and down, and up and down all the time."

"That may be, but I don't see how he could shake a whole town to pieces," said Jimmieboy, "unless he was a very heavy boy."

"He didn't weigh a bit more than you do," answered the picture. "He was heavy enough when he jumped to shake his nursery though, and the nursery was heavy enough to shake the house, and the house was heavy enough to shake the lot, and the lot was heavy enough to shake the street, and the street shook the whole town, and when the town shook, everybody thought there was an earthquake, and they all moved away, and took the name of the town with them, which is why I don't know where it was."

Jimmieboy was silent. He never knew before that not standing still could result in such an awful happening.

"I know another boy, too, who lived in—well, I won't say where, but he lived there. He broke a fine big mirror in his father's parlor by not standing still when he was told to."

"Did he shake it down?" asked Jimmieboy.

"No, indeed, he didn't," returned the picture. "He just stood in front of it and got so movey that the mirror couldn't keep up with him, but it tried to do it so hard that it shook itself to pieces. But that wasn't anything like as bad as what happened to Jumping Sam. He was the worst I ever knew. He never would keep still, and it all happened and he never could unhappen it, so that it's still so to this very day."

"But you haven't told me what happened yet," said Jimmieboy, very much interested in Jumping Sam.

"Well, I will tell you," said the picture, gravely. "And this is it. The story is a poem, Jimmieboy, and it's called:

"THE HORRID FATE OF JUMPING SAM.

"Small Sammy was as fine a lad
    As ever you did see ;
But one bad habit Sammy had,
    A Jumper bold was he.
And, oh ! his fate was very sad,
    As it was told to me.

"He never, never, would stand still
    In school or on the street ;
He'd squirm if he were well or ill,
    If on his back or feet.
He'd wriggle on the window-sill,
    He'd waggle in his seat.

"And so it happened one fine day,
    When all alone was he,
He got to jumping in a way
    That was a sight to see.
He leaped two feet at first, they say,
    And then he made it three.

"Then four, and five, the long day through,
    Until he could not stop.
Each jump he jumped much longer grew,
    Until he gave a hop
Up in the air a mile or two,
    A-twirling like a top.

"He turned about and tried to jump
    Back to his father's door,
But landed by the village pump,
    Some twenty miles or more
Beyond it, and an awful bump
    He'd got when it was o'er.

"And still his jumps increased in size,
    Until they got so great,
He landed on the railway ties
    In some far distant state:
And then he knew 'twould have been wise,
    His jumping to abate.

"But as the years passed slowly by,
    His jumping still went on,
Until he leaped from Italy,
    As far as Washington.
And he confessed, with heavy eye,
    It wasn't any fun.

" And when, in 1883,
    I met him up in Perth,
 He wept and said 'good-by' to me,
    And jumped around the earth.
 And I was saddened much to see
    That he knew naught of mirth.

" Last year in far Allahabad,
    Late in the month of June,
 I met again this jumping lad—
    'Twas in the afternoon—
 As he with visage pale and sad
    Was jumping to the moon.

" So all his days, leap after leap,
    He takes from morn to night.
 He cannot eat, he cannot sleep,
    But flies just like a kite,
 And all because he would not keep
    From jumping when he might.

" And I believe the moral's true—
    Though shown with little skill—
 That whatsoever you may do,
    Be it of good or ill,
 Once in a while it may pay you
    To practice keeping still."

A long silence followed the completion of the blurred picture's poem. For some reason or other it had made Jimmieboy think, and while he was thinking, wonderful to say, he was keeping very quiet, so that it was quite evident that the fate of Jumping Sam had had some effect upon him. Finally, however, the spell was broken, and he began to wiggle just as he wiggled while his picture was being taken, and then he said:

"I don't know whether to believe that story or not. I can't see your face very plainly here. Come over into the light and tell me the poem all over again, and I can tell by looking in your eye whether it is true or not."

The picture made no reply, and Jimmieboy, grasping it firmly in his hand, went to the window and gazed steadily at it for a minute, but it was useless. The picture not only refused to speak, but, as the rays of the setting sun fell full upon it, faded slowly from sight.

Nevertheless, true story or not, Jimmieboy has practiced standing still very often since the affair happened, which is a good thing for little boys to do, so that perhaps the brief life and long poem of the rejected picture were not wasted after all.

XI.

JIMMIEBOY AND THE BLANK-BOOK.

SOMEBODY had sighed deeply, and had said, "Oh dear!"

What bothered Jimmieboy was to find out who that somebody was. It couldn't have been mamma, because she had gone out that evening with papa to take dinner at Uncle Periwinkle's, and for the same reason, therefore, it could not have been papa that had sighed and said "Oh dear!" so plainly. Neither was it Moggie, as Jimmieboy called his nurse, companion, and friend, because Moggie, supposing him to be asleep, had gone up stairs to her own room to read. It might have been little Russ if it had only been a sigh that had come to Jimmieboy's ears, for little Russ was quite old enough to sigh; but as for adding "Oh dear!" that was quite out of the question, because all little Russ had ever been able to say was "Bzoo," and, as you may have observed for yourself, people who can only say "Bzoo" cannot say "Oh dear!"

It was so mysterious altogether that Jimmie-

"OH! DEAR!"

boy sat up straight on his pillow, and began to wonder if it wouldn't be well for him to get frightened and cry. The question was decided in favor of a shriek of terror; but the shriek did not come, because just as Jimmieboy got his mouth open to utter it the strange somebody sighed again, and said:

"Aren't you sorry for me, Jimmieboy?"

"Who are you?" asked Jimmieboy, peering through the darkness, trying to see who it was that had addressed him.

"I'm a poor unhappy Blank-book," came the answer. "A Blank-book with no hope now of

"EVERYBODY LAUGHED BUT ME."

ever becoming great. Did you ever feel as if you wanted to become great, Jimmieboy?"

"Oh, yes, indeed," returned the boy. "I do yet. I'm going to be a fireman when I grow up, and drive an engine, and hold a hose, and put out great configurations, as papa calls 'em."

"Then you know," returned the Blank-book, "or rather you can imagine, my awful sorrow

when I say that I have aspired to equally lofty
honors, but find myself now condemned to do
things I don't like, to devote my life not to great
and noble deeds, but to miserable every-day af-
fairs. You can easily see how I must feel if you
will only try to imagine your own feelings if,
after a life whose every thought and effort had
been directed toward making you the proud
driver of a fire-engine, you should find it necessary to settle down to the humdrum life of a law-
yer, all your hopes destroyed, and the goal
toward which you had ever striven placed far
beyond your reach."

"You didn't want to be a fireman, did you?"
asked Jimmieboy, softly.

"No," said the Blank-book, jumping off the
table, and crossing over to Jimmieboy's crib,
into which he climbed, much to the little fellow's delight. "No, I never wanted to be a fireman, or a policeman, or a car conductor, because I have always known that those were
things I never could become. No matter how
wise and great a Blank-book may be, there is a
limit to his wisdom and his greatness. It sometimes makes us unhappy to realize this, but
after all there is plenty in the world that a
Blank-book can do, and do nobly, without envy-

ing others who have to do far nobler and greater
things before they can be considered famous.
Everything we have to do in this world is worth
doing well, and everybody should be content to
do the things that are given to his kind to ac-
complish. The poker should always try to poke
as well as he can, and not envy the garden hose
because the garden hose can sprinkle flowers,
while he can't. The rake should be content to
do the best possible rake's work, and not sigh
because he cannot sing 'Annie Rooney' the way
the hand-organ does."

"Then why do you sigh because of the work
they have given you to do?"

"That's very simple," returned the Blank-book.
"I can explain that in a minute. While I have
no right to envy a glue-pot because it can hold
glue and I can't, I have a right to feel hurt and
envious when it falls to the lot of another Blank-
book, no better than myself, to become the
medium through which beautiful poems and
lovely thoughts are given to the world, while I
am compelled to do work of the meanest kind.

"It has always been my dream to become the
companion of a poet, of a philosopher, or of a
humorist—to be the Blank-book of his heart—to
lie quiet in his pocket until he had thought a

thought, and then to be pulled out of that pocket
and to be made the receptacle of that thought.

"Oh, I have dreamed ambitious dreams, Jimmieboy—ambitious dreams that must now re-
main only dreams, and never be real. Once, as
I lay with a thousand others just like me on the
shelf of the little stationery shop where your
mother bought me, I dreamed I was sold to a
poet—a true poet. Everywhere he went, went
I, and every beautiful line he thought of was
promptly put down upon one of my leaves with
a dainty gold pencil, contact with which was
enough to thrill me through and through.

"Here is one of the things I dreamed he wrote
upon my leaves:

> "'What's the use of tears?
>   What's the use of moping?
> What's the use of fears?
>   Here's to hoping!
>
> "'Life hath more of joy
>   Than she hath of weeping.
> When grief comes, my boy,
>   Pleasure's sleeping.
>
> "'Only sleeping, child;
>   Thou art not forsaken,
> Let thy smiles run wild—
>   She'll awaken!'

"Don't you think that's nice?" queried the Blank-book when he had finished reciting the poem.

"Very nice," said Jimmieboy. "And it's very true, too. Tears aren't any good. Why, they don't even wash your face."

"I know," returned the Blank-book. "Tears are just like rain clouds. A sunny smile can drive 'em away like autumn leaves before a whirl-wind."

"Or a clothes-line full of clothes before an east wind," suggested Jimmieboy.

"Yes: or like buckwheat cakes before a hungry school-boy," put in the Blank-book. "Then that same poet in my dream wrote a verse about his little boy I rather liked. It went this way:

"'Of rats and snails and puppy-dogs' tails
　　Some man has said boys are made;
But he who spoke to be truthful fails,
　　If 'twas of my boy 'twas said.

"'For honey, and wine, and sweet sunshine,
　　And fruits from over the swim,
And everything else that's fair and fine,
　　Are sure to be found in him.

"'His kisses are nice and sweet as spice,
　　His smile is richer than cake—
Which, if it were known to rats and mice,
　　The cheeses they would forsake.

"'His dear little voice is soft and choice,
    He giggles all day with glee,
And it makes my heart and soul rejoice,
    To think he belongs to me.' "

"That's first rate." said Jimmieboy. "Only Mother Goose has something very much like it about little girls."

"That was just it," returned the Blank-book. "She had been a little girl herself, and she was too proud to live. If she had been a boy instead of a girl, it would have been the boy who was made of sugar and spice and all that's nice."

"Didn't your dream-poet ever write anything funny in you?" asked Jimmieboy. "I do love funny poems."

"Well, I don't know whether some of the things he wrote were funny or not," returned the Blank-book, scratching his cover with a pencil he carried in a little loop at his side. "But they were queer. There was one about a small boy, named Napples, who spent all his time eating apples, till by some odd mistake he contracted an ache, and now with J. Ginger he grapples."

"That's the kind," said Jimmieboy. "I think to some people who never ate a green apple, or tasted Jamaica ginger, or contracted an ache, it would be real funny. I don't laugh at it, because I know how solemn Tommy Napples must have felt. Did you ever have any more like that?"

"Oh my, yes," returned the Blank-book. "Barrels full. This was another one—only I don't believe what it says is true:

> "'A man living near Navesink,
> Eats nothing but thistles and zinc,
>   With mustard and glue,
>   And pollywog stew,
> Washed down with the best of blue ink.'"

"That's pretty funny," said Jimmieboy.

"Is it?" queried the Blank-book, with a sigh. "I'll have to take your word for it. I can't laugh, because I have nothing to say ha! ha! with, and even if I could say ha! ha! I don't suppose I'd know when to laugh, because I don't know a joke when I see one."

"Really?" asked Jimmieboy, who had never supposed any one could be born so blind that he could not at least see a joke.

"Really," sighed the Blank-book. "Why, a man came into the store where I was for sale once, and said he wanted a Blank-book, and the clerk asked him what for—meaning, of course, did he want an account-book, a diary, or a copybook. The man answered, 'To wash windows with, of course,' and everybody laughed but me. I simply couldn't see the point. Can you?"

"Why, certainly," said Jimmieboy, a broad smile coming over his lips. "It was very funny. The point was that people don't wash windows with Blank-books."

"What's funny about that?" asked the Blank-book. "It would be a great deal funnier if people did wash windows with a Blank-book. He might have said 'to go coasting on,' or 'to sweeten my coffee with,' or 'to send out to the heathen,' and it would have been just as funny."

"I guess that's true," said Jimmieboy. "But it was funny just the same."

"No doubt," returned the Blank-book; "but it seems to me what's funny depends on the other fellow. You might get off a splendid joke, and if he hadn't his joke spectacles on he'd think it was nonsense."

"Oh no," said Jimmieboy. "If he hadn't his joke spectacles on he wouldn't think it was nonsense. Jokes are nonsense."

"But you said a moment ago the fun of the Blank-book joke was that you couldn't wash windows with one. That's a fact, so how could it be nonsense?"

"I never thought of it in that way," said Jimmieboy

"Ah!" ejaculated the Blank-book. "Now that is really funny, because I don't see how you could think of it in any other way."

"I don't see anything funny about that," began Jimmieboy.

"Oh dear!" sighed the Blank-book. "We never shall agree, except that I am willing to believe that you know more about nonsense than I do. Perhaps you can explain this poem to me. I dreamt my poet wrote this on my twelfth page. It was called 'A Plane Tale:'

> "'I used to be so surly, that
>   All men avoided me;
> But now I am a diplomat,
>   Of wondrous suavity.
>
> "'I met a carpenter one night,
>   Who wore a dotted vest;
> And when I asked if that was right,
>   He told me to go West.
>
> "'I seized his saw and brandished it,
>   As fiercely as I could,
> And told him, with much show of wit,
>   I thought he was no good.
>
> "'At that he looked me in the face,
>   And said my tone was gruff;
> My manner lacked a needed grace,
>   In every way was rough.

"'He seized and laid me on a plank,
    He gave a little cough ;
And then, although my spirits sank,
    He planed me wholly off !

"'And ever since that painful night,
    When he so treated me,
I've been as polished, smooth a wight,
    As any one can be.' "

"There isn't much sense in that," said Jimmieboy.

"Well, now, I think there is," said the Blankbook. "There's a moral to that. Two of 'em. One's mind your own business. If the carpenter wanted to wear a dotted vest it was nobody's affair. The other moral is, a little plane speaking goes a great way."

"Oh, what a joke!" cried Jimmieboy.

"I didn't make any joke," retorted the Blankbook, his Russia-leather cover getting red as a beet.

"Yes, you did, too," returned Jimmieboy. "Plane and plain—don't you see? P-l-a-n-e and p-l-a-i-n."

"Bah!" said the Blank-book. "Nonsense! That can't be a joke. That's a coincidence. Is that what you call a joke?"

"Certainly," replied Jimmieboy.

"Well, then, I'm not as badly off as I thought.

I wanted to be a poet's book and couldn't, but
it is better to be used for a wash-list as I am
than to help funny men to remember stuff like
that. I am very grateful to you, Jimmieboy, for
the information. You have made me see that
I might have fared worse than I have fared,

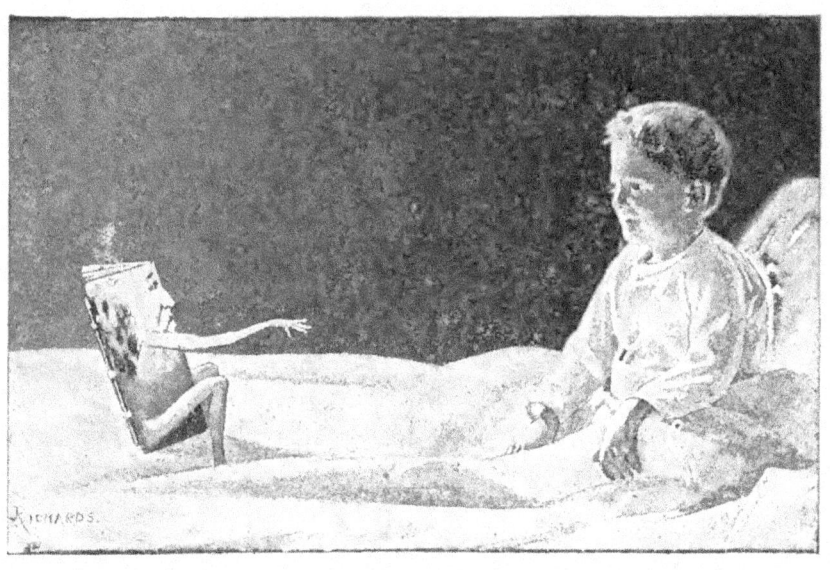

"IS THAT WHAT YOU CALL A JOKE?"

and I thank you, and as I hear your mamma and
papa coming up the stairs now, I'll run back to
the desk. Good-night!"

And the Blank-book kissed Jimmieboy, and
scampered over to the desk as fast as it could,
and the next day Jimmieboy begged so hard for

it that his mamma gave it to him for his very own.

"What shall you do with it now that you have it?" asked mamma.

"I'm going to save it till I grow up," returned Jimmieboy. "Maybe I'll be a poet, and I can use it to write poems in."

XII.

JIMMIEBOY AND THE COMET.

JIMMIEBOY was thinking very hard. He was also blinking quite as hard because he was undeniably sleepy. His father had been reading something to his mamma about a curious thing that lived up in the sky called a comet. Jimmieboy had never seen a comet, nor indeed before that had he even heard of one, so of course his ideas as to what it looked like were rather confused. His father's description of it was clear enough, perhaps, but nevertheless Jimmieboy found it difficult to conjure up in his mind any reasonable creature that could in any way resemble a comet. Finally , however, he made up his mind that it must look like a queer kind of a dog with nothing but a head and a tail—or perhaps it was a sort of fiery pollywog.

At any rate, while he thought and blinked,

what should he see peeping in at him through the window but the comet itself. Jimmieboy knew it was the comet because the comet told him so afterward, and besides it wore a placard suspended about its neck which had printed on it in great gold letters: "I'm the Comet. Come out and take a ride through the sky with me."

"Me?" cried Jimmieboy, starting up as soon as he had read the invitation.

Immediately the word "Yes" appeared on the placard and Jimmieboy walked over to the window and stepping right through the glass as though it were just so much air, found himself seated upon the Comet's back, and mounting to the sky so fast that his hair stood out behind him like so many pieces of stiff wire.

"Are you comfortable?" asked the Comet, after a few minutes.

"Yes," said Jimmieboy, "only you kind of dazzle my eyes. You are so bright."

The Comet appeared to be very much pleased at this remark, for he smiled so broadly that Jimmieboy could see the two ends of his mouth appear on either side of the back of his neck.

"You're right about that," said the Comet. "I'm the brightest thing there ever was. I'm all the time getting off jokes and things."

"Are you really?" cried Jimmieboy, delighted. "I am so glad, for I love jokes and—and things. Get off a joke now, will you?"

"Certainly," replied the obliging Comet. "You don't know why the moon is called she, do you?"

"No," said Jimmieboy. "Why is it?"

"Because it isn't a sun, so it must be a daughter," said the Comet. "Isn't that funny?"

"I guess so," said Jimmieboy, trying to look as if he thought the joke a good one. "But don't you know anything funnier than that?"

"Yes," returned the Comet. "What do you think of this: What is the only thing you can crack without splitting it?"

"That sounds interesting," said Jimmieboy, "but I'm sure I never could guess."

"Why, it's a joke, of course," said the Comet. "You can crack a joke eight times a day and it's as whole as it ever was when night comes."

"That's so," said Jimmieboy. "That's funnier than the other, too. I see now why they call you a Comic."

"I'm not a Comic," said the Comet, with a laugh at Jimmieboy's mistake. "I'm a Comet. I end with a T like the days when you have dinner in the afternoon. They end with a tea, don't they?"

"That's the best, yet," roared Jimmieboy. "If you give me another like that I may laugh harder and fall off, so I guess you'd better hadn't."

"How would you like to hear some of my poetry?" asked the Comet. "I'm a great writer of poetry, I can tell you. I won a prize once for writing more poetry in an hour than any other Comet in school."

"I'm very fond of it," said Jimmieboy. "Specially when it don't make sense."

"That's the kind I like, too," agreed the Comet. "I never can understand the other kind. I've got a queer sort of a head. I can't understand sense, but nonsense is as clear to me as—well as turtle soup. Ever see any turtle soup?"

"No," said Jimmieboy. "but I've seen turtles."

"Well. turtle soup is a million times clearer than turtles. so maybe you can get some idea of what I mean."

"Yes," said Jimmieboy. "I think I do. Nonsense poetry is like a window to you. You can see through it in a minute."

"Exactly," said the Comet. "Only nonsense poetry hasn't any glass in it, so it isn't exactly like a window to me after all."

"Well, anyhow," put in Jimmieboy. "Let's have some of the poetry."

"Very good," said the Comet. "Here goes. It's about an animal named the Speeler, and it's called 'The Speeler's Lament.'

"Oh, many years ago,
    When Jack and Jill were young,
There wandered to and fro,
Along the glistening snow,
    A Speeler, much unstrung.

"I asked the Speeler why
    He looked so mortal sad?
He gazed into my eye,
And then he made reply,
    In language very bad,

"'I'm sad,' said he, 'because
    A Speeler true I be;
And yet, despite my jaws,
My wings, and beak, and claws,
    Despite my manners free,

"'Despite my feathers fine,
    My voice so soft and sweet,
My truly fair outline,
My very handsome spine,
    And massive pair of feet,

"'In all this world of space—
    On foot, on fin, on wing—
From Nature's top to base,
There never was a trace
    Of any such strange thing.

> " 'And it does seem to me—
> Indeed it truly does—
> 'Tis dreadful, sir, to be,
> As you can plainly see,
> A thing that never was!' "

"What's a Speeler?" said Jimmieboy.

"It isn't anything. There isn't any such thing as a Speeler and that's what made this particular Speeler feel so badly," said the Comet. "I know I'd feel that way myself. It must be dreadful to be something that isn't. I was sorry after I had written that poem and created the poor Speeler because it doesn't seem right to create a thing just for the sake of making it unhappy to please people who like poetry of that kind."

"I'm afraid it was a sensible poem," said Jimmieboy. "Because, really, Mr. Comet, I can't understand it."

"Well, let me try you on another then, and take away the taste of that one. How do you like this. It's called 'Wobble Doo, the Squaller.

> "The Wobble Doo was fond of pie,
> He also loved peach jam.
> But what most pleased his eagle eye,
> Was pickled cakes and ham.

> "But when, perchance, he got no cake,
> Jam, ham, or pie at all,
> He'd sit upon a garden rake,
> And squall, and squall, and squall.

> "And as these *never* came his way,
>   This hero of my rhyme,
> I really do regret to say,
>   Was squalling all the time."

"Your poems are all sad, aren't they?" said Jimmieboy. "Couldn't you have let Wobble Doo have just a little bit of cake and jam?"

"No. It was impossible," replied the Comet, sadly, "I couldn't afford it. I did all I could for him in writing the poem. Seems to me that was enough. It brought him glory, and glory is harder to get than cakes and peach jam ever thought of being. Perhaps you'll like this better:

> "Abadee sollaker hollaker moo,
>   Carraway, sarraway mollaker doo—
> Hobledy, gobbledy, sassafras Sam,
>   Taramy, faramy, aramy jam."

"I don't understand it at all," said Jimmieboy. "What language is it in?"

"One I made up myself," said the Comet, gleefully. "And it's simply fine. I call it the Cometoo language. Nobody knows anything about it except myself, and I haven't mastered it yet –but my! It's the easiest language in the world to write poetry in. All you have to do is to go right ahead and make up words to suit yourself, and finding rhyme is no trouble at all when you do that."

"But what's the good of it?" asked Jimmieboy.

"Oh, it has plenty of advantages," said the Comet, shaking his head wisely. "In the first place if you have a language all your own, that nobody else knows, nobody else can write a poem in it. You have the whole field to yourself. Just think how great a man would be if he was the only one to understand English and write poetry in it. He'd get all the money that ever was paid for English poetry, which would be a fortune. It would come to at least $800, which is a good deal of money, considering."

"Considering what?" asked Jimmieboy.

"Considering what it would bring if wisely invested," said the Comet. "Did you ever think of what $800 was worth in peanuts, for instance."

Jimmieboy laughed at the idea of spending $800 in peanuts, and then he said: "No, I never thought anything about it. What is it worth in peanuts?"

"Well," said the Comet, scratching his head with his tail, "it's a very hard bit of arithmetic, but, I'll try to write it out for you. Peanuts, you know, cost ten cents a quart."

"Do they?" said Jimmieboy. "I never bought a

whole quart at once. I've only paid five cents a
pint."

"Well, five cents a pint is English for ten cents
a quart," said the Comet, "and in $800 there are
eight thousand ten centses, so that you could
get eight thousand quarts of peanuts for $800.
Now every quart of peanuts holds about fifty
peanut shellfuls, so that eight thousand quarts
of peanuts equal four hundred thousand peanuts
shellfuls. Each peanut shell holds two small
nuts so that in four hundred thousand of them
there are eight hundred thousand nuts."

"Phe-e-ew!" whistled Jimmieboy. "What a
feast."

"Yes," said tne Comet, "but just you wait.
Suppose you ate one of these nuts a minute, do
you know how long it would take you, eating
eight hours a day, to eat up the whole
lot?"

"No," said Jimmieboy, beginning to feel a little awed at the wondrous possibilities of $800 in
peanuts.

"Four years, six months, three weeks and six
days, and you'd have to eat Sundays to get
through it in that time," said the Comet. "In
soda water it would be quite as awful and in
peppermint sticks at two cents a foot it would

bring you a stick forty thousand feet, or more than seven miles long."

"Isn't $800 wonderful," said Jimmieboy, overcome by the mere thought of so much peppermint candy.

"Yes—but really I am much more wonderful when you think of me. You haven't been on my back more than ten minutes and yet in that time I have taken you all around the world," said the Comet.

"All the way!" said Jimmieboy.

"Yes," said the Comet, stopping suddenly. "Here we are back at your window again."

"But I didn't see China, and I wanted to," said the boy.

"Can't help it," said the Comet. "You had your chance, but you preferred to talk about poetry and peanuts. It isn't my fault. Off with you, now."

And then the Comet bucked like a wild Western Broncho, and as Jimmieboy went over his head through the window and landed plump in his papa's lap, the queer creature with the fiery tail flew off into space.

CHAPTER XIII.

JIMMIEBOY AND JACK FROST—IN WHICH JACK GIVES OFFENCE.

JIMMIEBOY is the proud possessor of a small brother, who, to use one of Jimmieboy's own expressions, is getting to be a good deal of a man. That is to say, he is old enough to go out driving all by himself, being eleven months of age, and quite capable of managing the fiery untamed nurse that pushes his carriage along the street. Of course, if the nurse had not been warranted kind and gentle when the baby's mamma went to find her in the beginning, little Russ would have had to have somebody go along with him when he went driving—somebody like Jimmieboy, for instance, to frighten off big dogs and policemen, and to see that the nurse didn't shy or run away—but as it was, the baby had developed force of character and self-reliance enough to go out unattended, and, except on one occasion, he got back again safe and sound.

This one occasion was early in December, when Nature, having observed that the great big boys had got through playing football and were beginning to think of snowballs, sent word to the Arctic Cold Weather Company that she desired to have delivered at once five days of low temperature for general distribution among her friends, which days were sent through by special messenger, arriving late on the night of December 1st, giving great satisfaction to everybody, particularly to those who deal in ice, ear-tabs, and skates. At first Jimmieboy's mamma thought that Nature was perhaps a little too generous with her frosty weather, and for two days she kept her two sons, Jimmieboy and Russ, cooped up in the house, laying in a supply of furnace and log-fire heat sufficiently large to keep them warm until the third day, when she thought that they might safely go out.

Upon the third day Jimmieboy's papa said that he imagined the boys were warm enough to venture out-of-doors, so they were bundled up in leggings, fur-lined coats, flannel bands, scarfs, silk handkerchiefs, lamb's-wool rugs, and "arctics," the door was opened, and out they went. Jimmieboy staid out seven minutes, and then came in again to see if he could find out why his nose had suddenly changed its color, first from pink to red, and then from red to blue. He also wished to come in, he said, because the

GAB.

JIMMIEBOY PREPARED FOR COLD WEATHER.

solid iron driver of his red express wagon had been "freezed stiff," and he was afraid if he staid out much longer he'd never thaw out again. Little Russ, on the contrary, lying luxuriously in his carriage, with no part of him visible save the tip end of his chin, which was so fat that the coverings would slip off, no matter how hard mamma and the nurse tried to make them stay on, remained out-of-doors for two hours, apparently very comfortable. His great blue eyes shone mirthfully when he came in, and until six o'clock that evening all went well with him, and then he began to whimper.

"What's the matter with my baby?" asked Jimmieboy.

Little Russ made no reply other than a grimace, which made Jimmieboy laugh, at which the

LITTLE RUSS.

baby opened his mouth as wide as he could and shrieked with wrath.

"I'm inclined to think," said the nurse, as she sought vainly to find where a possible pin might be creating a disturbance to the baby's discomfiture—"I'm inclined to think that perhaps he's got a pain somewhere."

And then the youthful Russ blinked his eyes, gave another shriek, and attempted to pout. Now it is a singular way little Russ has of pouting. He gets it from his mamma, who used to pout in just the same way when she was a little girl—so grandma says—and it consists entirely of sticking his chin out as far as he can, while concealing his lower lip as much as possible beneath the cherry-colored Cupid's bow that acts as his upper lip. A proceeding of this sort always results in making that chin the most conspicuous thing in the room, so that it is not surprising that when little Russ pouted every one in the room should at once notice that there was a great red spot upon it.

"Why, the poor little soul has been frost-bitten!" cried mamma, running for the cold cream —queer thing that, by-the-way, Jimmieboy thought. He would have put warm cream on a cold sore like that.

"So he is!" ejaculated papa, with an indignant glance at the chin, which only caused that fat little feature to pout the more. "Hadn't I better send for the doctor?"

"Does dogs frost-bite?" queried Jimmieboy, looking around the room for a stick with which to beat the dog that had done the biting, if perchance it was a dog that was responsible.

"No, indeed," said papa. "It wasn't a dog;

it was Jack Frost, and nobody else. He ought to be muzzled."

"Who is Jack Frost, papa?" Jimmieboy asked, so much interested in Jack that he for a moment forgot his suffering small brother.

"Jack? Why, Jack is a man named Frost, who deals in cold, and he goes around in winter biting people. He's a sort of iceman, only he's retired from trade, and gives things away, to people who don't want 'em. It would be better if he'd go into business, and sell his favors to people who do want 'em."

"Well, he's a naughty man," said Jimmieboy.

"Yes, indeed, he is," said papa. "Why, he's the man who withered all your mamma's plants, and painted our nice green lawn white; and then, when we wanted to dig holes for the fence posts, he came along and made the ground so hard it took all the edge off the spade, and made the hired man so tired that he overslept himself that night and let the furnace go out."

"Can't somebody catch him, and put him into prism?" asked Jimmieboy.

"Oh, he's been in prism lots of times," said papa, with a laugh at Jimmieboy's droll word; "but he manages to get out again."

"Where does he live, papa?" asked the boy.

"All around in winter. In summer he goes north for his health."

"And can't anybody ever get rid of him?"

"No. The only way to do that successfully would be to burn him out, and so far nobody has ever been able to do it entirely. You can put him out of your own house; but, if he wants to, he'll stay around the place and nip your plants, and freeze up your wells, and put a web of ice on your grass and sidewalks in spite of anything you can do."

By this time little Russ had quieted down and gone to sleep. The cold cream, aided by a huge bottleful of the food he liked best, which warmed up his little heart and various other parts of his being, to which the world had for a little while seemed bleak and drear, had put him in a contented frame of mind, and if the smile on his lips meant anything he had forgotten his woes in dreams of sweet and lovely things.

It was not so, however, with Jimmieboy, who grew more and more indignant as he thought of that great lumbering ice-man, Jack Frost, coming along and biting his dear little brother in that cruel fashion. It was simply cowardly, he thought. Of course Jimmieboy could understand how any one might wish to take a bite of some-

thing that was as sweet as little Russ was, and
when mosquitoes did it he was not disposed to
quarrel with them, because it was courageous in
a minute insect like a mosquito to risk his life
for his sweetmeats, but with Jack Frost it was
different. Why didn't he take a man of his size
like papa, for instance, or the grocer man? He
was afraid to—that was it—and so he fastened
upon a poor, helpless little man like Russ, only
eleven months old.

"He ought to be hitted on the head," said Jimmieboy.

"That wouldn't do any good," said papa. "It
wouldn't hurt him a bit. You couldn't kill him
with a hundred ice-picks, and I don't believe
even a steam-drill would lay him up more than a
week. What he's afraid of is heat—only heat,
and nothing else. That cracks him all up and
melts him, so that he can't bite anything."

Then Jimmieboy had his supper and began
playing with his toys until bedtime should come,
but all the time his mind was on that cruel Jack
Frost. Something else in the room was thinking
about it, too, only Jimmieboy didn't know it.
The little gas-stove that stood guard over by the
fire-place was quite as angry about Jack's behavior as anybody, but he kept very still until

along about eight o'clock when he began to sputter.

Jimmieboy stopped pushing his iron engine over the floor, and looked with heavy eyes at the gas-stove. This was extraordinary behavior for the stove, and Jimmieboy wondered what was the matter.

"Say!" whispered the stove, as Jimmieboy looked at him. "Let's get after that Frost fellow and make him wish he never was born."

Jimmieboy said nothing to this. He was too much surprised to say anything—the idea of a gas-stove speaking to him was so absurd. He only gazed steadfastly at the extraordinary thing in the fireplace, and then let his head droop down on his arms as he lay on the floor, and in a moment would have been asleep had not the stove again sputtered.

"Hi! Jimmieboy!" it cried. "Don't go to sleep. I know where Jack Frost lives, and we'll get after him and punish him for what he did to little Russ."

"How?" asked Jimmieboy, crawling across the room on his hands and knees, and looking earnestly at this strange gas-stove.

"Never mind how," returned the Stove. "I'll tell you that later. The point is, will you go? If

you will say the word I'll make all the arrange-
ments, and we'll set off after everybody has gone
to bed. It is a beautiful moonlight night.
Everything is just right for a successful trip.
There's enough snow on the ground for the sleigh
to move, and the river's all frozen over except
in the middle. We can skate as far as the ice
goes, and then, if there is no boat, we can put
on your papa's arctics, and walk across the water
to the other side. From there it's only a forty-
minute skate to Jack's home. He'll come in
about twelve o'clock, and we'll have him just
where we want him. What do you say?"

"I'll be in bed by the time you want to start,"
said Jimmieboy. "I'd like to do it very much,
but I don't know how to dress myself, and——"

"Never mind that," returned the Gas Stove.
"Go as you are."

"In my night-gown? On a cold night like
this?" queried the little fellow, more than ever
astonished at the Gas Stove's peculiarities.

"Why, certainly. I'll see that you are kept
warm," returned the stove. "I've got warmth
enough for twenty-six as it is, and if there's only
two of us— why, you see how it'll be. It'll be
too warm for two of us."

"That's so," said Jimmieboy. "I never

thought of it that way. I might sit on your lap if I couldn't keep warm any other way, eh?"

"I've got a better way than that," said the Stove, dancing a little jig on the tiles. "I'll get you a pair of gas gloves, some gas ear-tabs, a patent nose furnace, an overcoat lined with gas-jets that can be lit so as to keep you warm without burning you, and leggings, shoes, hats, and

THE GAS-STOVE TAPPED HIM LIGHTLY ON THE SHOULDER.

everything you need to make you feel as happy and warm as a poached egg on toast."

"That'll be splendid," said Jimmieboy. "I'll go, and we'll fix Jack so that he won't bite any of our people any more, eh?"

"Yes," said the Gas Stove, delighted at the prospect.

"Shall we muzzle him?" asked Jimmieboy. But the Gas Stove only winked, for just then mamma came up stairs from dinner, and as it was Jimmieboy's nurse's night out, his mamma undressed the little fellow, and put him in his crib, where he shortly dropped off to sleep.

In a little while everybody in the house had gone to bed, and when the last light had been extinguished the door of the room in which Jimmieboy slept was slowly opened, and the Gas Stove, all his lights turned down so that nobody could see him in the darkness, tiptoed in, and climbing upon the side of Jimmieboy's crib tapped him lightly on the shoulder.

"All ready?" he said, in a low whisper.

"Yes," answered Jimmieboy, softly, as he arose and got down on the floor. "How do we go? Down the stairs?"

"No," replied the Gas Stove. "We'll take the toy balloon up the chimney."

Which they at once proceeded to do.

XIV.

IN WHICH JIMMIEBOY AND THE GAS STOVE MAKE A START.

"NOW jump into the sleigh just as quickly as you can, Jimmieboy," said the Stove, as they issued forth into the cold night air. "Put on that fur cap and the overcoat, shoes, and gloves, and I'll light 'em up."

"They won't burn, for sure?" queried Jimmieboy, nervously, for the idea of wearing clothes heated by gas was a little bit terrifying.

"Not a bit," said the Stove in reply. "I wouldn't give 'em to you if they would. Thanks," he added, turning and throwing a ten-cent piece to a gas boy, who handed him the reins by which the horses were controlled. "We'll be back about sunrise."

"Very well," said the boy. "Do you want me turned on all night, sir?"

"No," answered the Stove. "Gas is expensive these days. You can turn yourself out right away. Have you fed the horses?"

"Yes, sir," said the boy. "They've each had four thousand feet by the meter for supper."

"Fuel or illuminating?" queried the Stove.

"Illuminating," replied the boy.

"THIS IS PRETTY FINE, EH?" SAID THE GAS-STOVE.

"Good," said the Stove. "That ought to make them bright. Good-by. Get up!"

With this the horses made a spring forward—fiery steeds in very truth, their outlines in jets, each burning a small flame, standing out like lines of stars in the sky.

"This is pretty fine, eh?" said the Gas Stove, with a smile, which, had any one looked, must

have been visible for miles, so light and cheerful
was it.

"Lovely!" cried Jimmieboy, almost gasping in
ecstasy. "I'm just as warm and comfortable as
can be. I didn't know you had a team like this."

"Ah, my boy," returned the Stove, "there's
lots you don't know. For instance:

> "You don't know why a fire will burn
>   On hot days merrily;
> And when the cold days come, will turn
>   As cold as I-C-E!
>
> "You don't know why the puppies bark,
>   Or why snap-turtles snap;
> Or why a horse runs round the park,
>   Because you say, 'git-ap.'
>
> "You don't know why a peach has fuzz
>   Upon its pinky cheek;
> Or what the poor Dumb-Crambo does
>   When he desires to speak.

"Do you?"

"No, I don't," said Jimmieboy. "But I should
like to very much."

"So should I," said the Stove. "We're very
much alike in a great many respects, and particularly in those in which we resemble each
other."

The truth of this was so evident that Jimmieboy could think of nothing to say in answer to it, so he merely observed: "I'm awful hungry."

This was a favorite remark of his, particularly between meals.

"So am I," said the Stove. "Let's see what we've got here. Just hold the reins while I dive down into the lunch basket."

Jimmieboy took the reins with some fear at first, but when he saw that they were high up in the air where there was really nothing but a star or two to run into, and realized that even they were millions of miles away, he soon got used to it, and was sorry when the Stove resumed control.

"There, Jimmieboy," said the Stove, as he drew his hand out of the basket. "There's a nice hot ginger-snap for you. I think I'll take a snack of this fuel gas myself."

"You don't eat gas, do you?" asked the small passenger.

"I guess I do," ejaculated the Stove, with a smack of his lips. "As our Gas Poet Laureate said:

"Oh, kerosene
Is good, I ween,
And so is apple sass;
But bring for me,
Oh, chickadee,
A bowl of fuel gas!

> "Some persons like
> The red beefstike,
> The cow just dotes on grass—
> But to my mind
> No one can find
> More toothsome things than gas.
>
> "And so I say,
> Bring me no hay;
> No roasted deep-sea bass.
> Bring me no pease,
> Or fricassees,
> If, haply, you have gas."

It's easy to eat, too," added the Stove. "In fact, I heard your papa say we consumed too much of it one day when he'd got his bill from the gas butcher."

"Do you chew it?" asked Jimmieboy.

"No, indeed. We take it in through a pipe. It isn't like soup or meat, though I sometimes think if people could take soup out of a pipe instead of from a spoon they'd look handsomer while they were eating. But the great thing about it is it's always ready, and if it comes cold, all you have to do is to touch a match to it, and it gets as hot as you could want."

"I should think you'd get tired of it," said Jimmieboy.

"Not at all. There's a great variety in gases.

There's fuel gas, illuminating gas, laughing gas, attagas——"

"What's that last?" queried Jimmieboy.

"Attagas? Why, when we want a game dinner, we have attagas. If you will look it up in the dictionary you will find that it's a sort of partridge. It's mighty good, too, with a sauce of stewed gasberries, and a mug or two of gasparillo to wash it down."

Here Jimmieboy smacked his lips. Gasparillo truly sounded as if it might be very delightful, though I don't myself belive it is any less bitter to the taste than some other barks of trees, such as quinine, for instance.

"Howdy do?" said the Stove, with a familiar nod to the east of them.

"Howdy do!" replied Jimmieboy.

"I wasn't speaking to you," said the Stove, with a laugh. "I was only nodding to an old friend of mine; he's got a fine place up in the sky there. His name is Sirius. They call him the dog-star, and all he has to do is twinkle. You can't see him all the time from your house, but when you get up as high as this he stands right out and twinkles at you. Pretty good fellow, Sirius is. I might have had his place, but somehow or other I prefer to work in-doors and rest nights. Sirius is out all the time, and has to keep awake all night. But we've got to get down to the earth again. Here's where we take to the skates."

Jimmieboy looked over the edge of the sleigh as the horses turned in response to a movement of the reins, and started down to earth. He saw a great white river below him, flowing silently along a narrow winding channel, everything on the border of which seemed bathed in silver except the middle of the river itself, a strip of forty or fifty feet in width, which was not frozen over.

"That's Frostland," whispered the Gas Stove. "We can't get over to the other side with this team because they are very skittish, and if the sleigh were overturned and our ammunition lost we should be lost ourselves. We've got to land directly below where we are now, skate to the edge of the ice on this bank, row over to the other, and then skate again directly to the palace. We mustn't let anybody know who we really are, either, or we may have trouble, and we want to avoid that; for you know, Jimmieboy,

> "The man who gets along without
>   A care or bit of strife,
>   Is certain sure, beyond all doubt,
>   To lead a happy life."

"But I can't skate," said Jimmieboy.

"You can slide, can't you?" asked the Stove.

"Yes, both ways. Standing up and sitting down."

"Well, my patent steam skates, operated by gas, will attend to all the rest if you will only stand up straight," returned the Stove, and the sleigh dropped lightly down to the earth, and the two crusaders against Jack Frost alighted.

"Isn't it beautiful here?" said Jimmieboy, as he looked about him and saw superb tall trees, their leaves white and glistening in the moonlight, bound in an icy covering that kept them always as he saw them then. "And look at the flowers," he added, joyously, as he caught sight of a bed of rose-bushes, only the flowers were lustrous as silver and of the same dazzling whiteness.

"Yes," said the Gas Stove, sadly. "Every time Jack Frost withers a flower or a plant he brings it here, and it remains forever as you see them now; he has had the choice of the most beautiful things in the world. But come, we must hurry. Put on these skates."

Jimmieboy did as he was told, and then the Stove lit a row of small jets of gas along the steel runners of the skates, and they grew warm to Jimmieboy's feet, and in a moment little puffs of steam issued forth from them, and Jimmieboy began to move, slowly at first, and then more and more quickly, until he was racing at breakneck speed.

"Hi, Stovey!" he cried, very much alarmed to find himself speeding off through this strange country all alone. "Hurry up and catch me, or I'll be out of sight."

"Keep on," hallooed the Stove in return. "Don't bother about me. I've got four feet to your two, and I can go twice as fast as you do. Keep on straight ahead, and I'll be up with you in a minute—just as soon as I can get the ammunition and my hose out."

"I wonder what he's going to do with the hose?" Jimmieboy asked himself. The Stove was too far behind him for the little skater to ask him.

"Halt!" cried a voice in front of Jimmieboy.

"I can't," gasped the little fellow, very much frightened, for as he gazed through the darkness to see who it was that addressed him, he perceived a huge snow man standing directly in his path.

"You must," cried the Snow Man, opening his mouth and breathing forth an icy blast that

nearly froze the water in Jimmieboy's eyes.
"You shall!" he added, opening his arms wide,
so that before he knew it Jimmieboy was pre-
cipitated into them.

"HALT!" CRIED A VOICE IN FRONT.

"See?" said the Snow Man. "I can compel
y——"

The Snow Man never got any further with this
remark, for in a moment Jimmieboy passed

straight through him. The heat of Jimmieboy's clothes had melted a hole through the Snow Man, and as the small skater turned to look at his adversary he saw him standing there, his head, his sides, and legs still intact, but from his waist down all the middle part of him had disappeared.

"Dear me! How sad," Jimmieboy said.

"Not at all," responded a voice beside him. "It serves him right; he's the meanest Snow Man that ever lived. If you hadn't melted him he'd have turned himself into an avalanche, and then you'd have been buried so deep in snow and ice you'd never have got out."

"Who are you?" queried Jimmieboy, with a startled glance in the direction whence the voice seemed to come.

"Only what you hear," replied the voice. "I am a voice. Jack Frost froze the rest of me and carted it away, and left me here for the rest of my life."

"What were you?"

"I cannot remember," said the voice. "I may have been anything you can think of. You could stand there and call me all the names you chose, and I couldn't deny that I was any of them.

"Sometimes I think I may have been
  A piece of apple pie ;
Perhaps a great and haughty queen,
Perhaps a gaily dressed marine,
  In former days was I.

"I may have been a calendar,
  To tell some man the date ;
I may have been a railway car,
A rocket or a shooting star,
  Or e'en a roller skate.

"I may have been a jar of jam,
  Perhaps a watch and chain ;
I may have been a boy named Sam,
An oyster or a toothsome clam,
  Perhaps a weather vane.

"I may have been a pot of ink,
  A sloop or schooner yacht ;
I may have been the missing link,
But *what* I was I cannot think—
  For I have quite forgot.

All I know is that I was something once; that
Jack Frost came along and caught me and added
me to his collection of curiosities, where I have
been ever since. They call me the invisible chat-
ter-box, and tell visitors that I escaped from the
National Vocabulary at Washington."

"I am very sorry for you," said Jimmieboy,
sympathetically.

"You needn't be," said the voice. "I'm happy :

I'm the only curiosity here that can be impudent to King Jack. I can say what I please, you know, and there's no way of punishing me; I'm like a newspaper in that respect. I can go into any home, high or low, say what I please, and there you are. Nobody can hurt me at all. Oh, it's just immense. I play all sorts of tricks

THE SNOW MAN.

on Jack, too. I get right up in front of his mouth and talk ridiculous nonsense, and people think he says it. Why, only the other night a Snow Man I don't like went in to see Jack, and Jack liked him tremendously, too, and was really glad to see him; but before the King had a chance to

say a word I hallooed out: 'Get out of here, you
donkey. Go make snowballs of your head and
throw them at yourself;' and the Snow Man
thought Jack said it, and, do you know, he went
outside and did it. He's been laid up ever
since."

"I think that was a very mean thing to do,"
said Jimmieboy.

"I'd agree with you if I had any conscience,
but alas! they've deprived me of that too,"
sighed the voice. "But look out," it added,
hastily. "Throw yourself into that snow-bank
or you'll fall into the river."

Without waiting to think why, Jimmieboy
obeyed the voice and threw himself headlong into
a huge snow bank at his side, and glanced anxiously about him.

He was indeed, as the voice had said, on the
very edge of the ice, and another yard's advance
would have landed him head over heels in the
rushing water.

"That would have been awful, wouldn't it?" he
said to the Stove, as his little friend came up.

"Yes, it would," returned the Stove. "It would
have put out the lights in your clothes, and that
would have been very awful, for I find we have
come away without any matches. Jump into the

boat, now, and row as straight for the other side as you can."

Jimmieboy looked about him for a boat, but couldn't see one.

"There is no boat," he said.

"Yes, there is—jump!" cried the Stove.

And Jimmieboy jumped, and, strange to relate, found himself in an instant seated amidships in an exquisitely light row-boat made entirely of ice.

"Row fast, now," said the Stove. "If you don't the boat will melt before we can get across."

XV.

IN THE HEART OF FROSTLAND.

"WE'RE afloat!
We're afloat!
In our trim ice-boat;
And we row—
Yeave ho!

"I guess I won't sing any more," said the Gas
Stove. "It's a hard song to sing, that is, particularly when you've never heard it before, and
can't think of another rhyme for boat."

"That's easy enough to find," returned Jimmieboy, pulling at the oars. "Coat rhymes with
boat, and so do note and moat and goat and——"

"Very true," assented the Stove, "but it
wouldn't do to use coat because we take our
coats off when we row. Note is good enough but
you don't have time to write one when you are
singing a sea-song. Moat isn't any good, because

nobody'd know whether you meant the moat of
a castle, a sun-moat, or the one in your eye.
As for goats, goats don't go well in poetry. So I
guess it's just as well to stop singing right here."

"How fast we go!" said Jimmieboy.

"What did you expect?" asked the Stove. "The
bottom of this boat is as slippery as can be, and,
of course, going up the river against the current
we get over the water faster than if we were
going the other way because we—er—because we
—well because we do."

"Seems to me," said Jimmieboy, "I'd better
turn out some of the gas in my coat. I'm melting right through the seat here."

"So am I," returned the Stove, with an anxious glance at the icy craft. "It won't be more
than a minute before I melt my end of the boat
all to pieces. I'm afraid we'll have to take to
our arctics after all. I brought a pair of your
father's along, and it's a good thing for us that
he has big feet, for you'll have to get in one and
I in the other."

Just then the stern of the boat melted away,
and the Stove, springing up from his seat and
throwing himself into one of the arctics, with
his ammunition and rubber hose, floated off.
Jimmieboy had barely time to get into the other

arctic when his end of the ice-boat also gave
way, and a cross-current in the stream catching
the arctic whirled it about and carried it and its
little passenger far away from the Stove who
shortly disappeared around a turn in the river,
so that Jimmieboy was left entirely alone in utter ignorance as to where he really was or what
he should do next. Generally Jimmieboy was
a very brave little boy, but he found his present
circumstances rather trying. To be floating
down a strange river in a large overshoe, with
absolutely no knowledge of the way home, and a
very dim notion only as to how he had managed
to get where he was, was terrifying, and when
he realized his position, great tears fell from Jimmieboy's eyes, freezing into little pearls of ice
before they landed in the bottom of the golosh.
where they piled up so rapidly that the strange
craft sank further and further into the water and
would certainly have sunk with their weight
had not the voice Jimmieboy had encountered a
little while before come to his rescue.

"Golosh, ahoy!" cried the voice. "Captain!
Captain! Lean over the side and cry in the river
or you'll sink your boat."

The sound of the voice was a great relief to the
little sailor who at once tried to obey the order

he had received but found it unnecessary since his tears immediately dried up.

"GOLOSH, AHOY!"

"Come out here in the boat with me!" cried Jimmieboy. "I'm awful lonesome and I don't know what to do."

"Then there is only one thing you can do," said the voice from a point directly over the buckle of the arctic. "And that is to sit still and let time show you. It's a great thing, Jimmieboy, when you don't know what to do and can't find any one to tell you, to sit down and do nothing, because if you did something you'd be likely to find out afterwards that it was the wrong thing. When I was young, in the days when I was what I used to be, I once read a poem that has lingered with me ever since. It was called 'Wait and See' and this is the way it went:

> " When you are puzzled what to do,
>   And no one's nigh to help you out;
>   You'll find it for the best that you
>   Should wait until Time gives the clew,
>   And then your business go about—
>   Of this there is no doubt.
>
> "Just see the cow! She never knows
>   What's going to happen next, so she
>   Contented 'mongst the daises goes,
>   In clover from her head to toes,
>   From care and trouble ever free—
>   She simply waits, you see!
>
> "The horse, unlike the cow, in fear
>   Jumps to and fro at maddest rate,
>   Tears down the street, doth snort and rear,

And knocks the wagon out of gear—
And just because he does not wait,
His woes accumulate.

"D. Crockett, famous in the past,
The same sage thought hath briefly wed
To words that must forever last,
Wherever haply they be cast :
'Be sure you're right, then go ahead,'
"That's what D. Crockett said.

Lots in that.   If you don't now what to do," continued the voice, "don't do it."

"I won't," said Jimmieboy.   "But do you know
where we are?"

"Yes," said the voice.   "I am here and you are
there, and I think it we stay just as we are forever there is not likely to be any change, so why
repine?   We are happy."

Just then the golosh passed into a huge cavern,
whose sides glistened like silver, and from the
roof of which hung millions of beautiful and at
times fantastically shaped icicles.

"This," said the voice, "is the gateway to the
Kingdom of Frostland.   At the far end you will
see a troop of ice soldiers standing guard.   I doubt
very much if you can get by them, unless you
have retained a great deal of that heat you had.
How is it?   Are you still lit?"

"I am," said Jimmieboy. "Just put your hand on my chest and see how hot it is."

"Can't do it," returned the voice, "for two reasons. First, I haven't a hand to do it with, and secondly, if I had, I couldn't see with it. People don't see with their hands any more than they sing with their toes; but say, Jimmieboy, wouldn't it be funny if we could do all those things—eh? What a fine poem this would be if it were only sensible:

" A singular song having greeted my toes,
    I stared till I weakened the sight of my nose
    To see what it was, and observed a sweet voice
    Come forth from the ears of Lucinda, so choice.

" I cast a cough-drop in the lovely one's eyes,
    Who opened her hands in a tone of surprise,
    And remarked, in a way that startled my wife,
    'I never was treated so ill in my life.'

"Then tears in a torrent coursed over her arms,
    And the blush on her teeth much heightened her
        charms,
    As, tossing the cough-drop straight back, with a
        sneeze,
    She smashed the green goggles I wear on my knees."

Jimmieboy laughed so long and so loudly at this poetical effusion that he attracted the attention of the guards, who immediately loaded their guns and began to pepper the invaders with snowballs.

"Throw yourself down on your stomach in the toe of the golosh," whispered the voice, "and they'll never know you are there. Keep perfectly quiet, and when any questions are asked, even if you are discovered, let me answer them. I can disguise myself so that they won't recognize me, and they'll think I'm your voice. In this way I think I can get you through in safety."

So Jimmieboy threw himself down in the golosh, and the voice began to sing.

> "No, no, my dear,
> I do not fear
> The devastating snow-ball;
> When it strikes me,
> I shriek with glee,
> And eat it like a dough-ball."

"Halt!" cried the ice-guards. "Who are you?"

"I am a haunted overshoe," replied the voice. "I am on the foot of a phantom which only appears at uncertain hours, and is consequently now invisible to you.

> "And, so I say,
> Oh, fire away,
> I fear ye not, icicles;
> Howe'er ye shoot,
> I can't but hoot,
> Your act so greatly tickles,"

"Shall we let it through?" asked the Captain
of the guards.

"I move we do," said one High Private.

"I move we don't," said another.

"All in favor of doing one thing or the other
say aye," cried the Captain.

"HALT!" CRIED THE ICE-GUARDS.

"Aye!" roared the company.

"Contrary-minded, no," added the Captain.

"No!" roared the company.

"Both motions are carried," said the Captain.
"We will now adjourn for luncheon."

The overshoe, meanwhile, had floated on down through the gates and was now out of the guards' sight and Jimmieboy sprang to his feet and looked about him once more, and what he saw was so beautiful that he sat speechless with delight. He was now in the heart of Frostland, and before him loomed the Palace, a marvelously massive pile of richly carven ice-blocks transparent as glass; and within, seated upon a throne of surpassing brilliance and beauty, sat King Jack surrounded by his courtiers, who were singing songs the like of which Jimmieboy never before had heard.

"Now remember, Jimmieboy," said the voice, as the overshoe with its passengers floated softly up to the huge snow-pier that ran out into the river at this point where they disembarked— "remember I am to do all the talking. Otherwise you might get into trouble."

"All right, Voicy," began Jimmieboy, and then there came a terrific shout from within.

"Who comes here!" cried King Jack, rising from his throne and pointing his finger at Jimmieboy.

"I am a traveling minstrel," Jimmieboy seemed to reply though in reality it was the kind-hearted voice that said it. "And I have come a thousand and six miles, eight blocks, fourteen feet, six inches to recite to your Majesty a poem I have written in honor of your approaching Jubilee."

"Have I a Jubilee approaching?" roared Jack, turning to his Secretary of State, who was so startled that his right arm melted.

"WHO COMES HERE?"

"Y—yes, your Majesty," stammered the Secretary, with a low bow. "It is coming along at the rate of sixty seconds a minute."

"Why have I not been informed of this before?" roared Jack, casting a glance at the cowering Secretary that withered the nose

straight off his face. "Don't you know that
Jubilees are useful to a man only because other
people give him presents in honor of the event?
And here you've kept me in ignorance of the
fact all this time, and the chances are I won't
get a thing—for I've neglected my relatives
dreadfully."

"Sire," pleaded the Secretary, "all that you
say is true, but I have attended to all that. I
have informed your friends that the Jubilee is
coming, and they are all preparing pleasant
little surprises for you. We are going to give
your Majesty a surprise party, which is the finest
kind of a party, because you don't have to go
home after it is over, and the guests bring their
own fried oysters, and pay all the bills."

"Ah!" said Jack, melting a little. "You are
a good man, after all. I will raise your salary,
and send your children a skating-pond on Christmas day; but when is this Jubilee to take
place?"

"In eight hundred and forty-seven years," returned the voice, who did not like the Secretary
of State, and wanted to get him in trouble.
"On the eighty-second day of July."

" What—a—at?" roared the King, glaring at
the Secretary.

"I didn't say a word, sire," cried the unfortunate Secretary.

"No?" sneered Jack. "I suppose it was I that answered my own question, eh? That settles you. The idea of my waiting eight hundred and forty-seven years for a Jubilee that is to take place on an impossible date! Executioner, take the Secretary of State out to the furnace-room, and compel him to sit before the fire until there's only enough of him left to make one snowball. Then take that and throw it at the most decrepit hack-driver in my domain. The humiliation of this delayer of Jubilees must be complete."

The Secretary of State was then led weeping away, and Jack, turning to the awed Jimmieboy, shouted out:

"Now for the minstrel. If the poem pleaseth our Royal Coolness, the singer shall have the position made vacant by that unfortunate snow-drift I have just degraded. Step right up, young fellow, and turn on the poem."

"Step up to the foot of the throne and make a bow, and leave the rest to me," whispered the voice to Jimmieboy. "All you've got to do is to move your lips and wave your arms. I'll do the talking."

Jimmieboy did as he was bade. He took up his

stand before the throne, bowed, and the voice began to declaim as Jimmieboy's lips moved, and his arms began to shoot out, first to the left and then to the right.

"This poem," said the voice, "is in the language of the Snortuguese, and has been prepared at great expense for this occasion, fourteen gallons of ink having been consumed on the first stanza alone, which runs as follows:

"Jack Frigidos,
Jack Frigidos,
Oh, what a trope you are!
How you do shine
And ghibeline,
And conjugate afar!"

"It begins very well, oh, minstrel!" said Jack, with an approving nod. "The ink was well expended. Mount thee yon table, and from thence deliver thyself of the remnant of thy rhyme."

"Thanks," returned the voice; "I will."

"Get up on the table, Jimmieboy," the voice added, "and we'll finish 'em off there. Be a little slow about it, for I've got to have time to compose the rest of the poem."

So Jimmieboy clambered up the leg of the table, and in a few moments was ready for the voice to begin, which the voice proceeded to do.

"I will repeat the first verse, your Majesty, for
the sake of completeness.   And here goes:

> "Jack Frigidos,
>   Jack Frigidos,
> Oh, what a trope you are!
>   How you do shine,
>   And ghibeline,
> And conjugate afar!
>
> "How debonair
>   Is thy back hair;
> Thy smile how contraband!
>   Would I could ape
>   Thy shapely shape,
> And arrogate thy hand!
>
> "That nose of thine,
>   How superfine!
> How pertinent thy chin.
>   How manifest
>   The palimpsest
> And contour of thy shin!
>
> "How ormolu
>   Thy revenue!
> How dusk thy silhouette!
>   How myrtilly
>   Thy pedigree
> Doth grace thine amulet!
>
> "What man is there,
>   Ay, anywere,
> What mortal chanticleer,

Can fail to find
Unto his mind
Thy buxom bandolier !

" Ah, Frigidos !
Jack Frigidos,
In parcel or in keg,
Another like
Thee none can strike
From Dan to Winnipeg."

Here the voice paused.

" Is that all?" queried Jack Frost.

" It is all I have written up to this moment," the voice answered. " Of course there are seventy or eighty more miles of it, because, as your Majesty is well aware, it would take many a league of poetry fitly to commemorate your virtues."

" Your answer is pleasing unto me," replied the monarch of Frostland, when the voice had thus spoken. " The office of the Secretary of State is yours. The salary is not large, but the duties are. They are to consist mainly of——"

Here the King was interrupted by a tremendous noise without. Evidently some one was creating a disturbance, and as Jimmieboy turned to see what it was, he saw the great ice mountain looming up over the far-distant horizon melt slowly away and dwindle out of sight; and then messengers, breathless with haste, rushed in and cried out to the King:

"We are attacked! we are attacked! A tribe from a far country, commanded by the Gas Stove, is even now within our boundaries, armed with a devastating hose, breathing forth fire, by which already has been destroyed the whole western frontier."

THE GAS-STOVE DESTROYING FROSTLAND.

"What is to be done?" cried Jack, in alarm, and springing to his feet. "Can we not send a regiment of cold winds out against them, and freeze them to their very marrows and blow out the gas?"

"We cannot, sire," returned the messenger, "for the heat is so deadly that the winds themselves thaw into balmy zephyrs before they reach the enemy."

"Not so!" cried the voice from Jimmieboy's lips. "For I will save you if you will place the matter in my hands."

"Noble creature!" sobbed Jack, grasping Jimmieboy by the hand. "Save my kingdom from destruction, and all that you ask of me in the future is yours."

And Jimmieboy, promising to help Jack, started out, clad with all the authority of his high office, to meet the Gas Stove.

XVI.

THE END OF THE STORY.

AS Jimmieboy proceeded along the icy road he observed that everything was beginning to thaw, and then, peering as far into the distance as he could, he saw a great flame burning fiercely and scorching everything with which it came in contact. It was quite evident that the Gas Stove had brought with him the most effective ammunition possible for his purposes.

"I don't see exactly how he does it," said the newly appointed Secretary of State, as he ran hurriedly toward the devastating fire.

"Easy enough," returned the voice. "He has brought along a large quantity of gas and a garden hose, and he has turned on the gas just as you would turn on water, lit it, and there you are. There is absolutely no withstanding him,

and unless he can be induced to stop very
shortly, he'll destroy this whole kingdom, and
we'll have nothing but a desert ocean; and I
can tell you, Jimmieboy, a desert ocean where
there is nothing but water is worse than a desert
desert where there is nothing but sand."

"It seems almost a pity to destroy such a
beautiful place as this," said Jimmieboy, looking
about him, taking note of the great tall ice-
covered trees and the frost flowers and grasses
at the road-side. "But, you know, Jack Frost bit
my little brother, which was very cowardly of
him, and that's why the Gas Stove and I have
come here to fight."

"I think you are wrong there," said the voice.
"I don't believe Jack any more than kissed him;
but if he did bite him, it was because he loved
him."

Jimmieboy had never thought of it in that
light before. All he knew was that whatever
Jack Frost had done, it had brought tears to little Russ's eyes and woe to his heart.

"It's rather a funny way to show love to bite
a person," said Jimmieboy.

"Just let me ask you a few questions,"
said the voice. "Do you like cherries and
peaches?"

"Oh, don't I!" cried Jimmieboy, smacking his lips. "I just dote on 'em!"

"Then," said the voice,

"Why do you bite the cherry sweet?
Why in the peach do your teeth meet?"

"Never thought of it that way," said Jimmieboy.

"I suppose not," returned the voice. "Are you fond of apples and gingerbread"

"Well, rather!" ejaculated Jimmieboy.

"Then tell me this," asked the voice:

"Why do you gnaw the apple red?
Why do you chew your gingerbread?"

"Because I like 'em," returned Jimmieboy.

"Why do you crunch your taffy brown?
Why do you nibble your jumble down?
Why do you munch your candy ball?
Why do you chew at all—at all?"

continued the voice.

"To make things last longer. 'Tain't proper to gulp 'em all down at once," answered Jimmieboy.

"And that's why Jack Frost bit little Russ," asserted the voice. "In the first place, he loved him. Little Russ was to him as sweet as a cherry is to you. In the second place, he took a little wee bite, because it wasn't proper to gulp him all down. To-morrow that bite spot will be well, and little Russ will be none the worst for it. Now I don't see why you should want to ruin all this beautiful country just for that. It isn't a crime to love babies or to eat cherries."

"That's so," said Jimmieboy. "But Jack Frost has done other things. He killed a lot of mamma's flowers."

"No, he didn't," returned the voice. "Your mamma left 'em out-doors all night, and Jack came along and did just what the bees do. He took all the sweetness he could find out of 'em, and brought them here, where he planted them and made them appear like flowers of silver. You see what the heat down there is doing?"

Jimmieboy looked, and saw the icy covering melting off the flowers and trees, and as the silver coating fell away they would wave softly in the balmy air for a moment, and then wither and crumble away.

"Isn't that too bad?" he said.

"It is, indeed," replied the voice. "Those flowers and trees would have stood and lived on forever in their ice coats—ever fresh, ever happy. The warmth from the invader's fire gives them one glad mad moment of ecstasy, and then they wither away, and are lost forever. Is that worth while, my boy?"

The voice quivered a little as it uttered these words, and Jimmieboy felt tears rising in is own eyes too. Jack Frost was not so bad a fellow, after all, as he had been made out.

"But he made our hired man's back ache when he went to dig some holes for the fence posts," said Jimmieboy, who now felt that he should have some excuse for his presence in Frostland, and on a mission of destruction. "Was that right of him?"

"Even if it was his fault. it was right," said the voice. "I don't believe it was his fault, though. Hired men have a way of having back-ache when there's lots to do. But supposing Jack did give it to him. That hired man was taking a spade and scarring Mother Earth with its sharp edge. Jack Frost gets all that he has from Mother Earth. She has given him work to do— work that has made him what he is—and it was his duty to protect her."

"Well, I don't know what to do," said Jimmie-boy, beginning to sob. "I came here for revenge, and I don't think——"

"There is only one thing for you to do, be true to those who trust you," said the voice. "Now who trusts you? Your nurse doesn't—she wouldn't let you out of her sight. Your papa believes in you, but he never would have intrusted such a mission as this to your hands; nor would your mamma or little Russ. On the other hand, Jack Frost has made you Secretary of State, and you promised to help him in this dreadful trial— *he trusts you.* As the poem says,

> "E'en though it's sure to take and bust you,
> Be ever true to them that trust you."

"I'll save them," said Jimmieboy. And then he started off on a run down the road, and ere long stood face to face with the Gas Stove. The latter immediately threw down his hose, turned off the gas, and clasped Jimmieboy to his heart.

"Saved! Saved!" he cried. "I have found you at last. Dear me, how anxious I have been about you!" And then he burst out in song:

> "But now, O joy?
> My averdupoy
> Will steadily increase;
> For, now you're back,
> My woes will pack
> Their clothes in their valise,
>
> "And fly afar,
> To the uttermost star
> That shines up in the skies,

While you and I
Will warble high
The gleesomest of cries.

"We'll sing and sing,
And warble and sing,
And warble, and sing, and sing,
And warble and sing,
And sing, sing, sing,
And warble and sing, sing, sing,"

"Come off!" ejaculated the voice. "That's mighty poor poetry for a Stove that's as glad as you are."

"Why, Jimmieboy, you pain me," said the Gas Stove, who thought that it was his little friend that had spoken. "I didn't think you would criticize my song of happiness that way."

"I never said a word," said Jimmieboy. "It was my friend the voice, who helped me when I was in trouble, and——"

"And by whose efforts," interrupted the voice, "our Jimmieboy here is now the Right Honorable Jamesboy, Secretary of State to his Majesty the Emperor of Frostland, Prince of Iceberg, Marquis Thawberry, and Chief Ice-cream Freezer to all the crowned heads of Europe, Asia, Africa, Austrilia and New Jersey. I'd advise you to take off your hat, Mr. Stove, for you are in the presence of a great man."

"No, no," cried Jimmieboy, as the Gas Stove doffed his iron lid; "don't take off your hat to me, Stovey. I am all that he says, but I am still Jimmieboy, and your friend."

"But what becomes of your war?" queried the Gas Stove, ruefully. "I can't fight against you, and you are a part of the government."

"That's a very sensible conclusion," said the voice. "Only I wouldn't let King Jack know that, or he wouldn't ever let Jimmieboy go away from here. What you want to do is to make terms that will be satisfactory to both parties, get Jack Frost to agree to 'em, and there you are. If he won't agree, the Gas Stove will have to go on with the war until he does agree."

"That's the thing to do, I suppose," said the Stove. "What shall I insist upon, Mr. Secretary"

"Well, I think Jack ought to quit biting babies, no matter if he does love 'em," said Jimmieboy.

"I insist upon it," said the Gas Stove, firmly.

"I think, too," said Jimmieboy, "that he ought not to run off with so many flowers."

"If you do not agree to that, Mr. Secretary," returned the Stove, "I shall turn on my canned devastation again."

"I shall endeavor to secure the King's consent," replied Jimmieboy. "And, furthermore, he must keep away from the water-pipes in my papa's house. He froze 'em all up last winter."

"That is my ultimatum," said the Stove.

"Your what?" queried Jimmieboy.

"My last word," explained the Stove.

"It's long enough to have been a half-dozen of your last words," laughed the voice. "But is that all you're to agree upon?"

"I don't know of anything more," said Jimmieboy.

"Nor I," said the Stove.

"You're a mean couple," ejaculated the voice, angrily. "If I had my way, you'd do something for one who has served you when you were in trouble," he added, addressing Jimmieboy. "Where would you have been if it hadn't been for—for—well, for a friend of mine?"

"I don't know who you mean," said Jimmieboy.

"He wants something for himself," whispered the Gas Stove, "and he is right."

"Oh, you don't know who I mean, eh?" sneered the voice. And then he added:

"Who saved you from the icy sea,
And brought you through S-A-F-E?
  Why, ME!

"Who thought about that jubilee,
   And filled Jack Frost chock up with glee?
         Why, ME!

"Who all your goings did o'ersee,
   And got this lofty place for thee?
         Why, ME!

"That's who. Now what are you going to do about it?"

THE GAS-STOVE IS INTRODUCED TO THE KING.

"He's going back to Jack Frost," said the Gas Stove, "and he is going to demand that you shall be made Secretary of State in his place, and he is going to tell Jack that if he ever removes you from that position I shall return and destroy the country."

"You are very moderate in your demands," said the voice. "I think King Jack will be very foolish if he refuses to acceede to them, particularly that one having reference to myself. I do not care for the office, of course, but since there seems to be a demand for me, I shall accept."

So Jimmieboy, followed by the Gas Stove and the voice, returned to the palace, and the demands of the Stove were laid before the monarch.

"I'll agree to 'em all gladly," said he, "save

THE GAS-STOVE BURNING MERRILY AND WINKING AT HIM FROM THE FIREPLACE.

that which forces me to deprive myself of your valuable services. Was he quite firm about that?"

"He was!" shouted the voice, before Jimmieboy could speak.

Here somebody else in the distance seemed to call: "Jimmieboy! Hi! Jimmieboy!"

"Shall I accede or stand by you?" asked Jack, taking Jimmieboy by the hand.

"You'd better accede," said Jimmieboy, looking around to see who was calling him, "for I have just heard some one calling me—my papa, I think—and I guess it's time for me to get up."

What Jack's response to this curious remark would have been no one knows, for just then a most strange thing took place. Jack Frost and his palace in an instant faded completely from view, and Jimmieboy in surprise closed his eyes, rubbed them with both his fists, and then opened them again, to find himself in his little cot in the nursery, the gas-stove burning merrily and winking at him from the fireplace, and the friendly voice, as usual, nowhere to be seen, and now not even to be heard.

No sole remnant of the frozen country remained, save a few beautiful frost pictures on the windows, which, it seemed to Jimmieboy, Jack had left there in remembrance of the services Jimmieboy had done him; and as for the frost kiss on little Russ's chin, it had become as invisible as that far sweeter kiss that mamma had placed upon that very same spot when she first discovered what Jack had done.

(THE END.)

Reprint Publishing

For People Who Go For Originals.

This book is a facsimile reprint of the original edition. The term refers to the facsimile with an original in size and design exactly matching simulation as photographic or scanned reproduction.

Facsimile editions offer us the chance to join in the library of historical, cultural and scientific history of mankind, and to rediscover.

The books of the facsimile edition may have marks, notations and other marginalia and pages with errors contained in the original volume. These traces of the past refers to the historical journey that has covered the book.

ISBN 978-3-95940-065-7

Made in Germany

www.reprintpublishing.com